THE PUBLICATIONS COMMITEE OF THE COUNCIL

Twentyfourth annual report of the Council of Missions

Cooperating with the Church of Christ in Japan

THE PUBLICATIONS COMMITEE OF THE COUNCIL

Twentyfourth annual report of the Council of Missions
Cooperating with the Church of Christ in Japan

ISBN/EAN: 9783741169298

Manufactured in Europe, USA, Canada, Australia, Japa

Cover: Foto ©Andreas Hilbeck / pixelio.de

Manufactured and distributed by brebook publishing software
(www.brebook.com)

THE PUBLICATIONS COMMITEE OF THE COUNCIL

Twentyfourth annual report of the Council of Missions

TWENTY-FOURTH

ANNUAL REPORT OF THE COUNCIL

OF MISSIONS

COÖPERATINGI WTII TIIE

CHURCH OF CHRIST IN JAPAN

ISSUED BY THE PUBLICATIONS COMMITTEE

OF THE COUNCIL

1901

Printed by THE FUKUIN PRINTING COMPANY, L'D.,
Yokohama, Japan.

OFFICERS OF THE COUNCIL
FOR 1901-1902

PRESIDENT.   .   E. Rothesay Miller
VICE PRESIDENT   .   Henry Stout
SECRETARY   . Albert Oltmans
TREASURER   .   John C. Ballagh

PUBLICATIONS COMMITTEE

William Imbrie
E. Rothesay Miller
M. N. Wyckoff
W. B. McIlvaine
T. M. MacNair
G. G. Hudson
H. K. Miller

SECRETARIES

OF THE

COÖPERATING MISSIONS

———

WILLIAM IMBRIE . . . TOKYO

WILLIAM YATES JONES . . . . FUKUI

M. N. WYCKOFF . . TOKYO

HENRY STOUT . . . . NAGASAKI

H. W. MYERS . TOKUSHIM

C. NOSS . . SENDAI

J. B. HAIL . WAKAYA

MISS MARTHA BERNINGER . YOKOHAM

CONTENTS

I. PROCEEDINGS OF THE COUNCIL.

1. OPENING AND SESSIONS OF THE COUNCIL.

2. REPORTS OF STANDING COMMITTEES:

1. Publications.
2. Sunday-school Literature.
3. Statistics.
4. Finances of the Council.

3. REPORTS OF SPECIAL COMMITTEES APPOINTED BY THE LAST COUNCIL:

1. General report of the work of the year.
2. Continuance and reinforcement of the Scotch Mission.
3. Ministerial relief.
4. Training of lay workers.
5. Distribution of forces.
6. Historical documents.

4. NEW BUSINESS:

1. Revision of the hymn-book.
2. Minute memorial of the Rev. Hugh Waddell and Mrs. A. K. Faust.

ROLL OF THE COUNCIL:

1. EAST JAPAN MISSION OF THE PRESBYTERIAN CHURCH IN THE U. S. A. (NORTHERN).
2. WEST JAPAN MISSION OF THE PRESBYTERIAN CHURCH IN THE U. S. A. (NORTHERN).
3. NORTH JAPAN MISSION OF THE REFORMED (Dutch) CHURCH IN AMERICA.
4. SOUTH JAPAN MISSION OF THE REFORMED (Dutch) CHURCH IN AMERICA.
5. MISSION OF THE PRESBYTERIAN CHURCH IN THE U. S. (SOUTHERN).
6. MISSION OF THE REFORMED (GERMAN) CHURCH IN THE U. S.
7. MISSION OF THE CUMBERLAND PRESBYTERIAN CHURCH.
8. WOMANS UNION MISSIONARY SOCIETY.

I.
PROCEEDINGS

TWENTY-FOURTH ANNUAL MEETING
OF THE COUNCIL

---

1. OPENING AND SESSIONS OF THE COUNCIL.

The Council of Missions Coöperating with the Church of Christ in Japan assembled in the Union Church, Karuizawa, at 10 a.m., on August 8th, 1901. The President, the Rev. T. C. Winn, preached the opening sermon, taking for his theme *Christianity the Ultimate Religion.*

The business session was opened with prayer by the Rev. E. S. Booth ; and the Secretary of the Council being absent, the Rev. A. Oltmans was appointed to take his place. The roll-call showed fifty-five members in attendance. All Presbyterian and Reformed missionaries from other countries present at Karuizawa, and also F. Parrott, Esq. of the Bible Societies Committee, were invited to sit as corresponding members.

The morning sessions of the Council each day were preceded by a prayer meeting from 8.30 till 9.

On the evening of the 9th a public meeting was held at which addresses were delivered by the Rev. C. A. Killie, Miss Russell and Miss Sheffield on their experiences at the time of the siege in Peking; and also by the Rev. W. Ashmore D.D. of Swatow on the political conditions in China.

All the meetings in the Union Church on Sunday were held under the direction of the Council. In the forenoon a sermon in English was preached by the Rev. F. S. Scudder, and one in the afternoon by the Rev. E. R. Miller in Japanese. In the afternoon also the Sacrament of the Lord's Supper was administered; the Rev. W. Y. Jones presiding, the Rev. II. W. Myers distributing the bread, and the Rev. J. E. Hail the wine.

On Monday a praise-meeting in which many participated was held, led by the Rev. E. R. Miller, President for the ensuing year. The opening address was made by Mr. Miller; a number of hymns were sung; and many references were made to the revival of interest in Christianity throughout the empire, and in particular in Tokyo. Among the special reasons for praise dwelt on by one or another were the following:—a. The Spirit of Christian unity manifest at the General Conference of Missionaries held in Tokyo, and later by various bodies of missionaries; and the readiness with which nearly all of the Churches united in the work of the Forward Movement (*Taikyo Dendo*). b. The promptness and efficiency with which so many of the laity participated in that movement. c. The fact that there are now throughout the empire so many organized churches ready to reap and care for the harvest. d. The number of schools and trained helpers

2

prepared to aid, and the heartiness with which the schools in Tokyo and elsewhere have already rendered aid. e. The fact that so many members of the Council and other missionaries are found in so many places in the empire able to guide and assist in the fuller instruction of the new converts and inquirers. f. The great advance in knowledge regarding the most effective methods to be followed both in beginning and carrying on evangelistic work; and especially the emphasis put upon united prayer by the churches accompanied by direct and didactic rather than indirect and apologetic preaching of the truths of Christianity. g. The increasing number of the sons and daughters of missionaries who have returned to Japan to share in the work of their fathers and mothers. h. The fact acknowledged by so many Japanese thinkers that the old religions are outworn, and that the nation is sorely in need of a new moral force such as can be found in Christianity alone. i. A general readiness to hear, and a condition of expectancy such as have not been seen for a decade. j. The joy of some to whom Christ has been revealed; a joy that should kindle other hearts also.

Besides praise for such blessings as these, earnest prayers were made that inquirers shall go on to fuller knowledge and stronger faith; that the danger of a reaction may be averted; that the indifference and opposition to be found in some parts of the country, notably in places like Fukui on the West Coast, may soon give way to a great spiritual awakening; and finally that special and constant prayer be offered by all for all missionaries and all Japanese workers alike.

3.

The business sessions of the Council closed on the afternoon of Saturday, the 10th.

2. REPORTS OF STANDING COMMITTEES.

Publications The following report of the Publications Committee* was read and adopted.

The twenty-third Annual Report of the Council was printed and distributed in the usual manner.

The following have been published by members of the Council:—A Sunday-school Hymnal, by Mrs. Jones and Miss Glenn ; A Service for Easter, by Mr. Scudder ; a tract entitled *Kami no Fukuin* (The Gospel of God) by Dr. Imbrie, and one entitled *Zensekai no Kami* by Mr. W. McS. Buchanan ; Missionary Statistics of the Tōhoku including a mission map, and also *Yūsha no Shūkyō*, a Tract for Soldiers, (second edition) by Mr. Noss ; *Katei Kyōiku*, a translation of Miss Harrison's Studies in Child Nature, by Mrs. Curtis ; A Catechism on the Confession of Faith of the *Nihon Kirisuto Kyōkwai* (Church of Christ in Japan), by Dr. Thompson ; A Devotional and Practical Commentary on the Book of Amos, by Dr. Alexander ; a second edition of A Catechism on the New Testament, by Mrs. McCauley ; What is Christianity ? by Dr. J. B. Hail ; *Fukuin Geppō*, a monthly four-page paper, by Mr. Brokaw ; *Yūkō*, a semi-monthly eight-page paper, by Mr. Jones ; *Yorokobi no Otozure* and *Chiisaki Otozure*, as hitherto, by Mrs. E. R. Miller. From March 1901 *Tōhoku Kyōkwai Jihō*, a monthly containing from four to eight pages, prepared by a committee of three primarily for the *Nihon Kirisuto Kyōkwai* in the Tōhoku.

With reference to the establishment of circulating libraries for the benefit of pastors and evangelists (see Twenty-third Annual Report of the Council, pg. 5), the Committee recommends the method adopted by the Mission

*Messrs. Imbrie, E. R. Miller, Wyckoff, Price, Landis, Snyder and Haworth.

of the (German) Reformed Church, and by the church in Kobe: viz. the establishment of such libraries in local centres.

The following report of the Committee on Sunday-school Literature was read and adopted.

The following publications have been issued by the Committee:

1. THE SUNDAY-SCHOOL MONTHLY for the use of teachers and advanced students. During half the year the MONTHLY was prepared by Dr. Albrecht, and during half by Mr. Landis. Each number contains from 70 to 90 pages. The price is to be raised from 30 to 40 *sen* per year.

2. THE INTERMEDIATE SCHOLARS QUARTERLY, prepared by Messrs. Draper and F. G. Harrington. The QUARTERLY is illustrated, and each number contains from 60 to 90 pages. The price is to be raised from 20 to 30 *sen* per year.

3. THE PRIMARY LEAFLET, a weekly prepared by Mrs. Thompson and Miss Cozad. The LEAFLET has been considerably enlarged; and the price is to be raised from 10 to 12 *sen* per year.

For the coming year Mr. Stanford will relieve Dr. Albrecht; Mr. C. K. Harrington, Mr. F. G. Harrington; and Miss Whitman, Mrs. Thomson.

The deficit for the past year amounts to about 1,200 *yen;* and owing to a change in the method of distributing any deficit, agreed to on an urgent representation on the part of members of the Baptist Mission, nearly one half of this deficit falls upon the Council. The advance in subscription rates however, as well as a probable increase in the number of subscriptions, will in all likelihood materially decrease the deficit for the coming year.

From an examination of the Sunday-school statistics as given in the Proceedings of the Tokyo Missionary Conference it appears that the number of Sunday-school scholars connected with the Church of Christ in Japan is only a little more than half of that of the church members; while in the case of the Methodists the reverse is true; i.e. the Sunday-school membership is almost twice the church membership. •

This state of things should lead to serious thought; showing as it does at least a comparative negligence in the performance of duty to the children both in and out of the churches, and along with that a certain lack of earnestness in systematic training in the study of the Bible. This is a matter affecting the Synod and the presbyteries no less than the Council. Normal training classes for teachers should be encouraged; and in many cases missionaries could perhaps do no better work than to form and guide such classes. Bible-women and others should do their utmost to bring in the children; and Bible classes for adults should be maintained in every church. Pastors and evangelists should understand that the Sunday-school is a part of the church, and a part of their care. Missionaries should make it a point to be present not only during the hour of service when they preach, but also during the session of the Sunday-school. Sunday-school conventions, as recently planned in Tokyo and elsewhere by Mr. Ikehara and others should be encouraged by the presence and active participation of teachers, pastors and missionaries alike.

Reference has already been made to the excellent Sunday-school Hymnal that has been issued by Mrs. Jones and Miss Glenn. This may be obtained at the Methodist Publishing House, Ginza, Tokyo. In various quarters the value of a Sunday-school paper has been urged. The Committee on Sunday-school Literature most cordially recommends the *Chiisaki Otozure* and the *Yorokobi no Otozure*. The former is prepared for the younger children; the latter is suited to the needs of the older ones as well as to those of many adults. Both are published on the 1st and the 5th of every month. The Committee is satisfied that nothing better can be wished for; and has made arrangements with Mrs. Miller to include these papers in the notices of Sunday-school literature sent out every autumn. Subscriptions may be sent to Mrs. E. R. Miller, Morioka, Iwate Ken.

The following resolutions were adopted :—

That the representatives of this Council on the Committee on Sunday-school Literature be instructed to urge upon the Synod, at its meeting in October, the importance of increased attention both to Sunday-schools and to Sunday-school literature.

That the Council recommends to the missions associated with it in the preparation of Sunday-school literature, that in the future the amount to be paid by the bodies represented in the work be in proportion to the membership of the Japanese Churches with which they coöperate, rather than to the number of missionaries (men) belonging to the bodies.

At the request of the Council, the Rev. J. C. R. Ewing, D.D. of India addressed the Council on the subject of Sunday-school literature in India.

The Committee on Statistics* presented its report which Statistics was adopted. A summary of it is presented in the tables on the following pages.

---

* Messrs. Noss. Landis, Winn, Pieters and Curtis.

MISSION STATISTICS

MISSION OF THE	MISSIONARIES					STATIONS	
	Men				Women	Stations where missionaries reside	Outstations
	Married		Unmarried		Unmarried		
	Ordained	Unordained	Ordained	Unordained			
Pres. Church in U.S.A. (North):							
East Japan Mission	6	1			9	5	31+
West Japan Mission	10				9	7	33
Total	16	1			18	12	64+
Refd. (Dutch) Church in A.:							
North Japan Mission	5	1			6	6	18
South Japan Mission	4		1		4	3	15
Total	9	1	1		10	9	33
Pres. Church in U.S. (South)	10				7	7	27
Refd. (German) Church in U.S.	7			1	3	3	40
Cumberland Pres. Church	5		1		6	5	?
Womans Union Miss. Society					5	1	6
Totals for 1900	47*	2*	2	1	49	37	170+
Totals for 1899	48	3	1	1	47	36	160 ?

* To these figures should be added 49, to include the number of wives; the whole number of missionaries connected with the Council being thus 150.

8

MISSION STATISTICS
(CONTINUED)
EDUCATIONAL WORK OF THE MISSIONS

MISSION OF THE	Theo. Schools	Students in Theo. Schools	Bible Training Schools	Students in Bible Schools	Boarding Schools for Boys	Pupils in Boarding Schools for Boys	Boarding Schools for Girls	Pupils in Boarding Schools for Girls
Pres. Church in U.S.A. (North):								
East Japan Mission	2	7	1	16	4	65	2	331
West Japan Mission							3	151
Total	2	6	1	16	4	65	5	482
Refd. (Dutch) Church in A.:								
North Japan Mission	4	5		1	4	65	1	61
South Japan Mission						98	1	50
Total	4	5		1	1½	163	2	111
Pres. Church in U.S. (South)	1	7					1	50
Refd. (German) Church in U.S.			1	12	1	84	1	68
Cumberland Pres. Church			1	30			1	60
Womans Union Miss. Society								53
Totals for 1900	2	17	3	59	3	312	11	824
Totals for 1901	3	18	3	7	3	322	11	721

* A yen is half a dollar in gold.

9

MISSION STATISTICS
(CONTINUED)
EDUCATIONAL WORK OF THE MISSIONS (CONTINUED)

MISSION OF THE	Day schools	Pupils in day schools	Christian pupils in all schools	Number professing Cristianity during year	Foreign teachers		Japanese teachers		Income from Japanese sources	Grants by Foreign Mission Bds. for Educ. work
					Men	Women	Men	Women		
Pres. Church in U.S.A. (North):									yen	yen
East Japan Mission	5	426	128	34	2	11	14	24	6400+	1300
West Japan Mission	6	342	86	19	2	7	13	27	2162	6098
Totals	11	768	214	53	2	18	27	51	8462+	19098
Refd. (Dutch) Church in A.:										
North Japan Mission			50	7	2	21	8	7	1125	?
South Japan Mission			23	11	2	21	13	4	?	4781
Totals			73	18	4	4	21	11	1125+	4781+
Pres. Church in U.S. (South)	?		?	?		1	2	3	800	1079
Refd. (German) Church in U.S.			59	21	2	2	16	8	?	1300
Cumberland Pres. Church			42	10		3	4	7	?	1433
Womans Union Miss. Society			35	?		1	8	16	?	5833
Totals for 1900	11	768	423+	102+	9	29	78	96	11387+	45224+
Totals for 1899	13	1159	338+	84?	11	32	85+	79+	?	37883+

MISSION STATISTICS
(CONTINUED)
EVANGELISTIC WORK OF THE MISSIONS

MISSION OF THE	Japanese ministers receiving salaries from missions	Salaries in yen	Itinerating of Japanese ministers in yen	Unordained Japanese preachers paid by missions	Salaries in yen	Itinerating of unordained preachers in yen	Bible women	Salaries of Bible women	Itinerating of Bible women	Grants by For. Miss. Bds. for Evang. work in yen
Pres. Church in U.S.A. (North):										
East Japan Mission	4	1068	?	10	3048	1654	22	2160	580	15100
West Japan Mission	8	2131	200	18	4248	210+	16	1014	214+	10052
Totals	12	3202	200+	28	7296	1264+	32	3174	794+	25152
Refd. (Dutch) Church in A. :										
North Japan Mission	4	1269	?	13	2514	?	3	285	?	6821
South Japan Mission	3	992	90	11	3121	583	1	122	?	?
Totals	7	2252	90+	24	5635	583+	4	417	?	6821+
Pres. Church in U.S. (South)	1	318	60	19	4809	?	6	600*	?	4247
Refd. (German) Church in U.S.	4	1620	240	21	4710	566	11	635*	150	9060
Cumberland Pres. Church	5	1500 ?	720 ?	7	1000 ?	600 ?	9	1080	?	8139
Womans Union Miss. Society							35	4342	482	5394†
Totals for 1900	29	8892 ?	1310+	99	23750 ?	3013+	97	10248 ?	1426+	62713
Totals for 1899	34	9415	?	113 ?	22591	1584	151 ?	?	?	39179+

* This may include the expenses of itinerating also.
† Includes the salaries of missionaries in evangelistic work.

11

STATISTICS OF THE CHURCH OF CHRIST IN JAPAN

PRESBYTERY	MEMBERSHIP Jan. 1: 1900				MEMBERSHIP Dec. 31: 1900				BAPTIZED			RESTORED		
	M.	W.	C.	Sum	M.	W.	C.	Sum	M.	W.	C.	M.	W.	C.
Miyagi	969	598	106	1673	1047	714	117	1878	101	52	15	39	40	13
Tokyo	2104	2217	659	4980	2144	2265	651	5060	120	101	32	78	57	
Naniwa	1342	1300	483	3125	1373	1338	519	3230	79	69	50	8	2	
Sanyo				510	167	188	107	504	6	3	2			
Chinzei				642	228	255	164	675	23	10	15			
Totals				10930				11347	329	235	114			

PRESBYTERY	RECEIVED FROM													
	Churches of other Presbyteries			Other churches of same Presbytery			Baptized in infancy and admitted to the Lord's Table		Other Churches					
	M.	W.	C.	M.	W.	C.	M.	W.	M.	W.	C.			
Miyagi	19	17	10	17	12	3	3	10	17	2	4			
Tokyo	27	20	12	17	29	5	4	2	7	20	1			
Naniwa	16	15	6	17	33	8	2	3		8				
Sanyo														
Chinzei	15						2	3						
Totals	15	18	14				25							

STATISTICS OF THE CHURCH OF CHRIST IN JAPAN
(CONTINUED)

PRESBYTERY	DISMISSED TO											Deceased		
	Other churches of same Presbytery			Churches of other Presbyteries			Other Churches							
	M.	W.	C.	M.	W.	C.	M.	W.	C.			M.	W.	C.
Miyagi	29	21	8	6	3	3	6	1				11	4	1
Tokyo	28	28	16	17	34	8	23	17	13			33	44	8
Naniwa	24	38	7	25	16	16	10	15	1			31	16	
Sanyo			8	10								6	1	5
Chinzei			6	9	11							2	2	2

PRESBYTERY	Excommunicated		Names erased from church register			Ceased to commune		Resident elsewhere			Residence unknown		
	M.	W.	M.	W.	C.	M.	W.	M.	W.	C.	M.	W.	C.
Miyagi	1	7	20	8	11	19	5	326	212	29	16	8	21
Tokyo	6	6	125	61	4	30	18	685	654	117	126	102	5
Naniwa	4	1	5	7	1	10	5	553	381	121	23	16	
Sanyo				5			1	46	42	30	7		
Chinzei	2	1	10	6		5	3	104	104	61	7	8	5

STATISTICS OF THE CHURCH OF CHRIST IN JAPAN

(CONTINUED)

PRESBYTERY	Actual attendance at the Lord's Supper			Average attendance at Sunday service		Average attendance at prayer-meeting		SUNDAY-SCHOOLS					Teachers	
								Scholars				Average attendance		
	M.	W.	Sum	M.	W.	M	W.	Boys	Girls	M.	W.		M.	W.
Miragi	615	431	1046	384	282	132	92	460	589	69	52	322	54	48
Tokyo	1228	1441	2669	332	872	340	326	847	967	159	203	672	119	94
Naniwa			1705	515	545	242	262	491	627	279	284	430	79	90
Sanyo								87	121	60	78	854	16	9
Chinzei								100	101	47	48		16	14
Totals								1985	2405	614	665		284	255

PRESBYTERY	CONTRIBUTIONS				EXPENDITURES					Value of church property	Endowment funds
	To Board Home Missions	To other objects	Sum of contributions	Received from missions	Salaries Pastors and Evang.	Evangelistic expenses	Charities	Current expenses	Occasional and special expenses		
Miragi	yen 163.	4297.	4460.	5724.	6271.	492.	556	1859.	1091.	5945.	311.
Tokyo	692.	13965.	14657.	2982.	8765.		225	4761.	2171.	13514.	4595.
Naniwa	309.	10197.	10506.	4817.	7752.		102	2916.	3793.	35500.	3717.
Sanyo	86.	1105.†	1191.	?	?			?			
Chinzei	136.	2881.	3017.	?	2745.			?			
Totals	1386.*	32445.	33831.								

* This includes only the contributions to the *Dendo Kyoku* (Board of Home Mission) by the churches as churches. In addition to this individual church members contribute directly to Board. The receipts from both sources amounted to about yen 3530.
† This probably includes grants from the *Dendo Kyoku*.

14

STATISTICS OF THE CHURCH OF CHRIST IN JAPAN
(CONTINUED)
SUMMARY OF PRINCIPAL ITEMS COMPARED WITH THOSE OF 1899

PRESBYTERY	Membership	Received on confession	Sunday school scholars	Contributions to Ind. Home Missions *	Contributions to other objects	Average per member — Contributions to Id. Home Mission 1899	1900	Average per member — Contributions to other objects 1899	1900	Ministers full members of Presbytery †	Missionaries advisory members of Presbytery ‡	Lay Preachers §	Churches	Communities of believers
Miyagi	1878	155	1272	163.	4297.	.083	.087	2.11	2.25	17	6	13	7	27
Tokyo	5060	236	2389	692.	13865.	.084	.137	2.47	2.76	29	4	40	31	37
Naniwa	3230	152	1850	309.	10197.	.103	.696	2.71	3.19	18	15	17	16	22
Sanyo	504	9	351	86.	1105.	7	.171	3.29	2.11	5	7	8	6	10
Chinzei	675	38	326	136.	2881.	.24	.202	2.13	4.20	5	4	15	7	7
Totals	11347	585	6188	1386.	32345.	.69?	.122	2.47	2.86	74	33	93	71	113
Totals 1899	10930	700	5907	1100.?	26654.		.024		.41	81	26	109		
Increase	417		281	286.	5811.						7	16		
Decrease	114													

* See note under preceding table.

† Including subordinates who have joined Presbyteries by letter.

‡ For the sake of subordinates cooperating with the Church of Christ in Japan, but who are unable to enter Presbyteries in the usual way by letters of dismission from the other Presbyteries, the following provision is made:—Canon 25 § 6. Advisory Members: Ministers who sincerely accept the Constitution, Canons and Confession of Faith, and who sincerely cooperate in the work of the Church of Christ in Japan, but who are unable to apply for admission under Canon 14, may be admitted as Advisory Members by a two-thirds vote. Advisory Members may speak, introduce resolutions, and be elected to serve on committees, but no committee shall have a majority of Advisory Members. Presbyteries having four or less than four Advisory Members shall elect one as an Advisory Member of the Synod.

Those having eight shall elect two; those having twelve, three.

§ Lay-preachers are men regularly licensed by a Presbytery to preach the gospel. They shall labor under the direction of the Presbytery or of each ministers as the Presbytery shall appoint to their oversight. Constitution, Art. 7.

¶ As here employed, the term means companies of baptized believers not yet organized as churches, but under the direct care of a Presbytery and whose names are enrolled in a register kept by the Clerk of the Presbytery. Canon 1.

The Treasurer of the Council presented the Financial Report for the year. The report was referred to an Auditing Committee,* who examined the same and reported it correct with a debit balance of 150.33 *yen*. The report was adopted.

3. Reports of special committees appointed by the last Council.

The General Report of the Work of the Year† was read by Dr. J. B. Hail. A resolution was adopted thanking Dr. Hail, and directing that a thousand copies of the report be printed.

The Committee‡ appointed to express to the Board of Foreign Missions of the United Free Presbyterian Church of Scotland the appreciation by the Council of the work of the Mission of the United Presbyterian Church in Japan, and to urge that the mission be continued and reinforced, reported that in answer to its letter it had received a reply from the Rev. James Buchanan stating that the way was not clear to comply with the request of the Council. Following is the correspondence:—

Tokyo, Sept. 17th, 1900.

To the Board of Foreign Missions
of the United Free Church.

Dear Brethren:
At the recent Annual Meeting of the Council of Missions Coöperating with the Church of Christ in Japan,

---

* Messrs. Brokaw and Price.
† See II. following the Proceedings of the Council.
‡ Messrs. Imbrie, Booth and Winn.

16

we were appointed a committee to express to you the esteem in which the work of the Japan Mission of the United Presbyterian Church is held by the Council, and to urge that the mission be continued and reinforced.

You have no doubt already received, through the Rev. Hugh Waddell, a communication addressed to you by the ministers and elders of the Church of Christ in Japan residing in the City of Tokyo.

The Council entertains the same feelings that are so cordially expressed in that letter regarding the work of the U. P. Mission now so long continued. It has earnestly hoped that the union of the Free and United Churches might open the way to an increase in the number of missionaries from Scotland: and it learns with deep regret that, on the contrary, there is a likelihood that the mission may be discontinued.

There was a time, some years ago, when it seemed to many that with the close of the century it might no longer be necessary to send reinforcements from home; but neither the missions nor the thoughtful men among the Japanese Christians have now any such expectation. There is little reason to doubt that a strong force of missionaries will be needed in Japan for at least a generation to come.

Certain indeed it is that Christianity has obtained a footing in Japan. The progress made is perhaps unprecedented in the history of modern missions. There are many Christians among the Japanese; and the evidence that Christianity is becoming more and more a leaven in the nation is increasingly clear to every intelligent and careful observer. But none the less is it true that there is a population of nearly fifty millions, to which Christianity is little on nothing more than a name. As the Japanese ministers and elders say to you, " It is manifest that the Church of Christ in Japan must undertake the toils of a long siege; and, for the right performance of that work, it needs and must have the help of the Churches of Christ in other lands."

For several years therefore the conviction has been

17

strengthening in the minds of the members of the Council that important centres not yet occupied should be occupied, and that to do this the force of missionaries connected with it should be increased.

Accordingly a resolution to that effect was adopted at the meeting of the Council held last year, and the matter was put into the hands of a special committee. That committee, after a careful survey of the field, agreed that there are twenty places that ought to be occupied by the Council; of which only six have in them resident missionaries belonging to any Church whatever. The report of this committee was adopted at the recent meeting of the Council; and action was taken to urge the subject upon the attention of all of the Boards of Foreign Missions represented in the Council.

We therefore beg of you to give the matter your careful consideration. It would give to the Council a pleasure beyond what you think to learn that you are ready to occupy one or two of the twenty places already referred to. Four or even two missionaries from you would bring new strength and new inspiration.

In what we have thus far said we have had in mind only the needs of Japan itself. But may we not rightly add that at this time, when Japan is entering upon a new career of influence in Asia, there are peculiar reasons why the Churches of Christ in England and Scotland and America should renew their efforts to hasten the day when Christianity shall become one of its controlling forces?

The call in itself is imperative; and now when in the providence of God the Churches in America have had laid upon them new and pressing responsiblities, we feel that we may urge the matter upon you with special insistence.

With Christian regards,

Sincerely yours,

WILLIAM IMBRIE.

T. C. WINN.

E. S. BOOTH.

To the Rev. William Imbrie, D.D.,
Tokyo, Japan.

Dear Dr. Imbrie,
I duly received your letter of the 28th September enclosing communication from the Council of Japan Missions. I have laid these documents before our Committee and they have unanimously agreed to intimate to you that they do not see their way to re-open the question which was settled by the United Presbyterian Synod previous to the Union.

I suppose you are aware that the Board, acting under instructions from the Synod, have terminated their work in Japan. They were influenced in this course by the following among other considerations:—(1) That they had only two missionaries in Japan, both of whom were in impaired health; (2) that there are upwards of a hundred missionaries in Tokyo, the greater number of whom are from American Churches and societies; and (3) that the resources of the Church are fully required to meet the growing demands of the other mission fields in which the United Presbyterian missionaries are almost the sole workers.

We shall never cease to take a warm interest in the progress of mission work in Japan, and trust that the large body of missionaries who are in that country will find that their labors are being blessed with an abundant success.

With kindest regards,

Yours very sincerely,

JAS. BUCHANAN.

The Committee on Ministerial Relief* reported progress, Ministeria relief
and the Council instructed the committee to formulate its plan without waiting for action on the part of the Synod.

---

* Messrs. Pieters, Wyckoff and J. B. Hail.

The Committee on the Training of Lay Workers* presented the following report which was adopted :—

Replies to the inquiries of the Committee have been received from a considerable number of the members of the Council. From these replies it appears :—(1) That the importance of enlisting lay workers is generally recognized, and that efforts are being more or less vigorously made in that direction. (2) That, with a few exceptions, no very large or definite results are reported ; but that the recent *Taikyo Dendo* movement has shown the existence of much latent energy that might be and ought to be used. (3) That most activity has been shown where the Japanese pastors or evangelists have encouraged and guided. (4) That Sunday-school workers are few, and that many of those who do engage in Sunday-school work are insufficiently instructed in the Scriptures, and otherwise inefficient. (5) That methods have been various and not usually the result of definite plans.

It seems to your Committee that lay workers can be enlisted in direct evangelistic work if their interest and sympathy can be aroused ; and that while this must be done chiefly by Japanese leaders, missionaries can lend very effective aid.

The Committee was continued for another year.

The Committee on Distribution of Forces† reported the following resolution which was adopted :—

That the Council appoint a Committee of Advice consisting of one member from each of the constituent missions, to which may be presented requests or recommendations from any of the missions regarding the opening of new stations, or the locating of missionaries ; said committee to take the initiative in offering advice should it think proper to do so.

* Messrs. S. P. Fulton, Wyckoff and J. C. Ballagh.
† Messrs. MacNair, Winn, E. R. Miller, Peeke, S. P. Fulton, Schneder and J. B. Hail.

In connection with the above the following additional resolution was adopted:—

That the Council instructs the Committee on Distribution of Forces to communicate with the several missions of the Council; and in case the missions consent to allowing this committee to adjust forces in the field in cases of special need, even to the temporary placing of a member or members of one mission in the field of another, the committee shall seek the consent of the Boards with which the missions composing this Council are connected, to the exercising of the above mentioned power.

The Committee on Historical Documents* reported that it had collected most of the Annual Reports of the Council; and that it requests members of the Council to send to it copies of the Reports issued prior to 1897, as well as any other documents of historical value to the Council or the Church of Christ in Japan.

Historical documents

4. NEW BUSINESS.

The Secretary of the Committee on the Revision of the Japanese Hymn-book presented the matter to the Council, and the following resolutions were adopted:—

Revision of the hymn-book

1. That in accordance with precedent in similar joint enterprises, the share of the expenses incurred in connection with the Union Japanese Hymnal now in preparation, that would otherwise be met by the Missions of the Presbyterian Church in the U.S.A. and the Reformed Church in America, be paid by the Council through its Treasurer.

2. That the Council recommends to the Committee on the Revision of the Japanese hymn-book that any assess-

* The Secretary of the Council, the Librarian of the Meiji Gakuin, and Dr. Imbrie.

ment upon the missions (or groups of missions) of expenses incurred in the preparation of the new hymn-book be based upon the membership of the Japanese churches with which the missions (or groups of missions) coöperate.

The late Rev. Hugh Waddell and Mrs. A. K. Faust

The following minute in memory of the late Rev. Hugh Waddell and Mrs. A. K. Faust was presented by the committee* appointed to prepare it, and was adopted by the Council with the direction that copies of it be sent to the families of the deceased and to the Boards or missions with which they were connected.

By a singular Providence we are called upon to record at the same time the death of one of the oldest and one of the youngest members of this Council: the Rev. Hugh Waddell of the United Free Presbyterian Church of Scotland, who came to Japan in 1874; and Mrs. A. K. Faust, a member of the Mission of the Reformed Church in the United States, who arrived in 1890.

It was with sorrow that we first heard of Mr. Waddell's failing health after returning to the home land, and with a feeling of personal loss that we learned by a recent mail that he had "fallen on sleep" in the City of Belfast, Ireland.

Mr. Waddell was one of those who took part in the formation of the Church of Christ in Japan; and he continued in sympathetic work with and for that Church through all its history until he was obliged to leave on account of ill health just when the Board of Foreign Missions of the United Presbyterian Church had decided to discontinue its mission to Japan. We would assure the Board with which he was so long connected, as well as his family, of our sympathy with them in their loss, and of our prayers for their comfort through the Holy Spirit. May the seed of the Gospel which our friend and fellow laborer sowed broad-cast throughout the land, still bear

* Messrs. E. R. Miller and W. E. Lampe.

fruit a hundred fold to the glory of God and the well-being of Japan.

It is also with sincere regret that we record the early death of Mrs. Faust before she had fully entered into the work for which she was so eminently fitted and to which she was so thoroughly consecrated. She has been called by her Saviour to sit at his feet, to look into his face, and to learn of him; and even now her sweet memory is gently leading those to whom she had devoted her life to that Saviour she so loved and honored. Being dead she yet speaketh. We extend our heartfelt sympathy to her husband in his sorrow, and to the Mission of the Reformed Church in its loss. May we all be ready to meet her with the Saviour in his kingdom.

A resolution was adopted to the effect that in connection with the Annual Meeting in 1902 the Council hold a conference of two days for the consideration of topics pertaining to the spiritual side of the work of the missions.

Conference in connection with the Annual Meeting in 1902

A committee was appointed to prepare a program for such a conference. The report of the committee with some changes was adopted by the Council and referred to a special committee* to complete the program presented and to make all necessary preparation for carrying it out.

Following is the list of topics as at present arranged :—

FIRST DAY.

MORNING: Christ as a Personal Worker.

1. What the Bible teaches on the personal preparation of Christ.
2. What the Bible teaches on the methods of work used by Christ.

---

* Messrs. E. R. Miller, Jones and McIlvaine.

AFTERNOON: Personal Preparation of Missionaries.

1. Bible teaching on personal preparation.
2. Bible teaching on leading difficulties to the missionary worker personally.

SECOND DAY.

MORNING: Conditions of the Field.

1. What does the Bible say about the nature of the field?
2. Practical experiences.

AFTERNOON: Missionaries as workers with the Japanese.

1. What is our relation to the Japanese workers?
2. How can we be most helpful to our Japanese brethren?

EVENING: Praise and consecration meeting, the President of the Council presiding.

Reply to Dr. Ewing regarding the union of Pres. and Refd. Missions and Churches in Japan The Rev. J. C. R. Ewing, D.D., President of Forman Christian College, Lahore, India, informed the Council regarding a proposition to form in India a union of Presbyterian and Reformed missions similar to that of the Council; and, with a view to bringing the reply of the Council to the attention of those in India interested in the matter, submitted the following questions:—

1. Has the union of Churches in Japan resulted in increased interest on the part of the home Churches in the work in this country?

2. Has the union stimulated the Japanese Church to greater effort in the way of making the gospel known to the Japanese people?

A committee was appointed to frame a reply to these questions. The report of the committee was adopted and placed in the hands of Dr. Ewing. In substance it was as follows :—

The union of Presbyterian and Reformed missionaries and churches in Japan was formed in 1877. At that time it embraced the missionaries of the Presbyterian Church in the U.S.A., of the Reformed (Dutch) Church in America, and of the United Presbyterian Church of Scotland ; together with the Japanese churches more or less closely connected with them. In 1883 the Reformed (German) Church in the U.S., and in 1885 the Presbyterian Church in the U.S., established missions in Japan. Both of these missions cordially, and with the full consent of the churches which they represent, entered the union and were assigned to the special of care particular sections of the empire, one in the north and the other in the south. Still later in 1889 the mission of the Cumberland Presbyterian Church, and in 1892 that of the Womans Union Missionary Society, both of which had long been at work in Japan, were welcomed to membership in the union. During the past year, greatly to the regret of the Council, it has lost the Scotch mission from its roll, That however is due solely to the fact that the United Presbyterian Church has felt constrained to withdraw altogether from Japan, in order to concentrate its efforts upon other mission fields. Turning now to the specific inquiries made by Dr. Ewing :—

1. When the plan was originally proposed that all the Presbyterian and Reformed missions in Japan should unite their efforts to establish one Japanese Church not to be ecclesiastically connected with any foreign church, the objection was definitely raised by some at home that the result would be a diminution of interest on the part of the churches at home in the work in Japan. In fact that fear has proved to have been entirely groundless. It has not in the least lessened the zeal of the Boards of Foreign Missions to do all in their power for the furtherance of the

25

gospel in Japan. If the combination of forces has made it possible to do more work than could otherwise be accomplished, the vastness of the work still undone must for a long time to come remain a complete answer to any proposition to reduce the force or the appropriations. So far as the congregations at home are concerned, it is the common experience that nothing excites greater interest or warmer approval than the fact that there is in Japan but one Presbyterian or Reformed Church instead of six. Add to this the fact that since the union was first formed, and when there had been time to observe its working, the missions of three churches and one missionary society have entered the union. That could hardly be if the feeling at home were that the plan of union is injurious to the interest of the churches at home. Nor, if such an effect were apparent, would the various Methodist missions in Japan now be planning for the formation of a similar union among themselves.

2. Since the Japanese church has been one from almost the very beginning, it is difficult to answer the second question with perfect precision. It may however fairly be said that the fact that the church is one and that it extends over most of the empire has developed a sense of church unity and also a sense of responsibility for the evangelization of the whole nation, that would otherwise certainly have been less pronounced. The special interest of the church in evangelistic work is apparent in its Board of Home Missions, which derives its income almost wholly from contributions by the Japanese churches and individual Christians.

The following resolutions were adopted :—

That in the opinion of the Council the publication of a Religious Review in connection with the several missions constituting this Council is desirable, and that the question of publishing such a periodical be referred to the Publications Committee with power to act in case the several missions approve and guarantee an adequate support.

That the Council recommend to the several Boards Recommendation regarding statistics with which the missions are connected the acceptance of the Council statistics in the place of statistics prepared by the separate missions.

That copies of such publications as may be issued by Exhibition of new publications members of the Council during the year be placed on exhibition at the next meeting of the Council.

The Council having learned of the death of the mother The late Mrs. Price of the Rev. H. B. Price, special prayer was offered in behalf of the sorrowing family.

Messrs. Booth and Landis were appointed the Com- Committee of Arrangements mittee of Arrangements for the next meeting of the Council.

The Rev. H. M. Landis was appointed to prepare the Report of Work of the Year next General Report of the Work of the Year.

The thanks of the Council were returned to the Rev. Thanks of the Council to the President T. C. Winn, the retiring President, for his faithful and efficient services; and he was requested to offer a copy of his sermon to the *Fukuin Shimpo* for publication.

The thanks of the Council were returned to the Karui- Thanks to the Karuizawa Church zawa Church for the use of its building and other courtesies.

On the recommendation of the Committee on Nomina- Officers and committees tions, the following appointments for the coming year were made:—

President, E. Rothesay Miller; Vice President, Henry Stout; Secretary, A. Oltmans; Treasurer, J. C. Ballagh.

Publications Committee: William Imbrie, E. Rothesay Miller, M. N. Wyckoff, W. B. McIlvaine, T. M. Mac-Nair, G. G. Hudson, H. K. Miller.

27

Committee on Distribution of Forces: T. M. MacNair, T. C. Winn, E. Rothesay Miller, H. V. S. Peeke, S. P. Fulton, D. B. Schneder and J. B. Hail.

Committee on Statistics: H. M. Landis, T. C. Winn, A. Pieters and J. W. Doughty.

Next annual meeting The Council adjourned to meet in Karuizawa, at 10 a.m., on Thursday, the 24th of July, 1902.

Close of the Council After singing the Doxology the Council adjourned.

II.

GENERAL REPORT OF THE WORK OF THE YEAR.

BY THE

Rev. J. B. Hail, D.D.

The Table of statistics of Christian and Missionary Work for the Year 1900 compiled by the Rev. H. Loomis shows that there are 750 Protestant, 209 Roman Catholic and two Greek Missionaries in Japan. The Protestant missionaries occupy 157 stations, the Roman 95 and the Greek 2. The Roman and Greek missions occupy 72 stations in common with Protestant missions. Protestant missions occupy 82 stations where there are no Roman or Greek missionaries. Roman missionaries occupy 23 towns where there are no Protestant missionaries. In all, there are 29 stations where missionaries connected with this Council reside. Twenty-one of these stations are occupied in common with other missions, eight by Presbyterians alone. The whole number of missionaries of all bodies residing in the 29 towns and cities is 535.

The large cities are, as a matter of course, best manned. The City of Tokyo is occupied by 175 Protestant missionaries representing 31 societies or churches; the City of Osaka by 50 missionaries representing 11 societies; Yokohama by 36 missionaries representing 11 societies; Kobe by 47 missionaries representing 8 societies; Sendai by 32 missionaries representing 6 societies; Kyoto by 22 missionaries representing 5 societies; Nagoya by 21 missionaries representing 5 societies.

In all there are 180 stations where missionaries reside. As the statistics of 1899 give 308 cities, towns, and villages with populations of over 10,000, it seems that there are 128 of these without a resident missionary.

There are two movements among the missions and Japanese churches which have been emphasized during the year under review. One is the movement toward Christian union. From the beginning of the missionary work in Japan there has been a movement in the direction of union. This Council and the Church of Christ in Japan, the Sei Kyokwai and the College of Bishops; and now the completion of the plans for consolidating the work of the various Methodist missions, and forming only one Methodist Church, as well as various general enterprises such as publishing Sunday-school literature, tract publication, hymn-books produced by joint committees, are fruits of this movement. During the year under review this movement has been greatly stimulated, first in the direction of bringing the Japanese churches into more intimate relations; secondly in bringing the missions closer together and thirdly in bringing missions and Japanese churches nearer together.

The Evangelical Alliance, organized more than twenty years ago, at its triennial meeting in the City of Osaka last year, resolved to attempt the evangelization of Japan in the first year of the twentieth century.

The year 1900 from May on to the end of the year was spent in preparation for this great forward movement. This preparation consisted in enlisting all the churches in union work. Many of the churches were making special preparation independently. The committee of the Evangelical Alliance addressed itself to the harmonizing of all the movements so that there should be no labor lost but that the whole Christian power in the empire might be directed to the best advantage. Its efforts were also directed towards full spiritual equipment, and the raising of funds for pushing the work.

30

On the initiation of this Council "A General Conference of Evangelical Protestant Missions in Japan" was called to convene in Tokyo on the 24th day of October 1900. The committee planned to emphasize the spiritual side of the programme. The Conference met according to the call and spent eight days in a most harmonious discussion of missionary work and plans. The three great results of this Conference were first, enlightenment; second, a great spiritual uplift or revival; and third, a great impetus towards unity or union. The Conference by a unanimous note adopted the following resolution :—

This Conference of Missionaries, assembled in the City of Tokyo, proclaims its belief that all those who are one with Christ by faith are one body; and it calls upon all those who love the Lord Jesus and his Church in sincerity and truth to pray and to labor for the full realization of such a corporate oneness as the Master himself prayed for on that night in which he was betrayed.

In accordance with the spirit of this resolution a Promoting Committee was appointed to draft a constitution for a Standing Committee of Coöperating Christian Missions in Japan. This committee has already sent to the various missions as the result of its work the Constitution* of the Proposed Standing Committee of Coöperating Christian Missions in Japan. This constitution is to go into effect when such a number of missions as include in their membership not less than two-thirds of the Protestant missionaries in Japan shall have signified their acceptance of the same in writing to the Secretary of the Promoting Committee. In the mean time meetings have been held; and circular letters and forms of prayer for union printed and circulated, in pursuance of this object.

A committee from the Evangelical Alliance, asked the privilege of presenting its plans for a forward movement to the General Conference of Missionaries. This request was gladly granted and the Conference heartily seconded the plans and recommended the missionaries to coöperate

* See Appendix I.

in pushing the work. As a result all the Protestant Churches and missionaries in Japan with but a very few exceptions have from the beginning of the year 1901 been brought into the closest and most harmonious relations, and have stood shoulder to shoulder and heart to heart in the great work of evangelizing Japan. The result of this movement so far is the greatest religious awakening Japan has yet witnessed. Tokyo is the center of this great revival work but reports from Nagoya, Kyoto, Osaka, Kobe, Kyushu in the west and south, and Sendai and other places in the north show that there is a wide-spread and deep religious interest all over the land.

This awakening has shown itself first in the quickening of the spiritual life of the churches; and secondly in the training of lay members in Christian work. Prayer meetings have grown in interest and attendance. Pastors and evangelists have developed greatly along evangelistic lines. The preaching has been direct and evangelical. The general testimony is that Christ has been the theme of all sermons as never before. Great numbers of people have attended the services held in all parts of the cities above mentioned and in many of the more important towns. Churches, public halls, and theatres have been crowded with quiet and attentive audiences; and those who have given their names as desiring Christian instruction are counted by thousands in Tokyo and Yokohama, and by hundreds in other cities.

The churches are making preparations to take up the work again in the fall and expect even greater things from God.

The second is a movement on the part of the Educational Department of the Government to a more liberal attitude toward Christian schools.

Every young man in Japan is liable to conscription for three years service in the army when he reaches the age of twenty. Students in government schools and in schools recognized by the government as doing the work of government schools are exempted from this service until the age of twenty-eight. They are then required to serve only for one year, and are also eligible to promotion. Also all students in government Middle Schools and schools approved by the the Minister of Education as doing the work of the Middle Schools were admitted to the Higher Schools on presenting their certificates of graduation. By order of the Minister of Education schools in which religious instruction was given were excluded from these privileges. Our Christian schools were thus forced to give up their privileges or their religious instruction. They gave up the privileges. This has now been changed, so that Christian schools notwithstanding their Christian instruction may be recognised by the Minister of Education, and the students exempted from military service and also admitted to the Higher Schools on passing a competition examination which is now required of the graduates of the government schools also.* This gives the Christians schools a free field, which is all they have asked or could ask. As a result of this new departure they all show a better attendance then last year.

_____ __ __ _ ___

* See Appendix II.

SUPPLEMENT.

REPORTS RECEIVED FROM MEMBERS OF THE MISSIONS.

1. East Japan Mission of the Presbyterian Church in the U. S. A. (Northern).

STATION.	POPULATION.	FU OR KEN.	POPULATION.
Tokyo	1425366	Tokyo Fu	2075694
Yokohama	193762	Kanagawa Ken	916356
Otaru	15897 ⎫		
Sapporo	37464 ⎬ Hokkaido		3869300
Asahigawa	15000 ⎭		

Dr. Thompson:—"My own work during the past year has been the general care or supervision of work in churches and preaching places in Tokyo; in Urawa, Hachioji, Kirin, Ashikaga; and in Utsunomiya to the north of this city. Most of the places just mentioned have been without stationed Evangelists or regular visitation; and they have done as well as it is reasonable to expect under the circumstances. Some have done better than others. The work at Kirin and in the vicinity is encouraging. In Hachioji too which is regularly visited we see no reason to be cast down. Elsewhere as at Urawa, Utsunomiya and Ashikaga difficulties have been encountered which cannot be readily overcome, the work there accordingly languishes.

Since the great evangelistic movement began on May 12th and before, I have been much engaged in the Shinsakae Church. This continues only during the absence of Mr. Okuno, the acting pastor, who is now absent in the north. In this church from May 12th to June 2nd during the evening meetings more than twenty men and women gave in their

34

names and announced their purpose to consider the claims of Christianity. Since the meetings have been discontinued these inquirers have called for not a little pastoral care visitation and instruction, and will require more before being prepared for admission to the Church. The majority of them are employees in the various factories around Tsukiji. They have only two rest days in the month, the 1st and the 15th. Besides this they have to work until eight o'clock at night. Knowing this we can see why it is that difficulty is encountered and may be expected in collecting them in classes on the Sabbath or any other day for religious instruction. On the whole we have been agreeably disappointed since the meetings every evening were discontinued, and instruction classes for enquirers, were formed to observe the number and evident sincerity of those who have thus far attended. How many will persevere to the end remains to be seen; but if three-fourths or more prove to be wayside or stony ground hearers or seed sown among thorns, we still have good reason to thank God for this awakening. At Tsunohazu, another point under my care, more than seventy responded to the various calls made on the hearers during the meetings to decide to at least investigate the claims of Christ.

The experience in these two places shows us how necessary and advantageous it is in a movement of the kind under consideration, and at all times if possible, to have faithful station workers. At Shinsakae the Bible woman and her son have done most of the hard work in visiting inquirers and keeping up meetings for their instruction. At Tsunohazu too there are a faithful evangelist and his wife who have done and do about all that is done. I earnestly wish we had the means of increasing the number of such."

DR. IMBRIE :—It is quite clear that there is now in Japan a widespread revival of interest in Christianity. How is to be accounted for? How deep is it? What are its permanent results to be? are questions constantly asked; but the fact in general cannot be denied. It has become so evident, that the Japanese press is seeking and publishing information regarding it, and leading articles appear that are no doubt suggested by it. This interest is manifest in many parts of Japan; but in what I now write I confine myself chiefly to Tokyo, where I have had opportunities for personal observation and direct inquiry.

The first attempt in Tokyo was one to awaken a general interest in the movement among all the Christians in the city. To do this, public meetings and in particular union prayer meetings were held. That attempt however though carried on for some time produced few apparent results, either within or without the churches. One reason at least for this failure lay in the fact that the distances in Tokyo are very great and at that stage of the movement it was not possible to get the Christians generally to attend the meetings.

The next step was to select a particular district of the city, known as Kyobashi Ku, and to concentrate effort upon it. New methods also, of which I will speak presently, were adopted. At the outset the interest shown was not marked, but within a few days it was sufficient to attract the attention of the Christian community, and after a fortnight it commanded it. At the end of seventeen days the special work in Kyobashi Ku was suspended in order to transfer efforts to other districts. There are now (in June) three centres of operation in the city; the same methods are pursued and the same results follow.

Some years ago when the general interest in Christianity was so marked, it was common to hold great meetings in theatres and large halls. Thus far such meetings have not been held in Tokyo. Instead of this the plan is to hold meetings every night in all the churches in the particular district of the city in which special work is carried on, and in every church a band of volunteers is organized, whose members pledge themselves to pray morning and evening for the guidance and blessing of God, to attend all the meetings and to see that the various methods adopted to attract persons to the evening meetings are faithfully carried on. Thus the local church, as an organization, is made the centre from which effort proceeds and into which results are to be gathered.

In order to attract hearers to the evening meetings various means are employed. Placards are posted in hotels, barber shops, bath-houses, and other public places. These placards are about fifteen inches wide and twenty inches long. The most attractive one to my mind is one with a light blue background, the upper third of which is occupied by two white flags, crossed. One is the Japanese flag with its red rising sun in the centre, and the other for its centre has a red Greek cross. The two flagstaffs are caught together with a red and black silk cord and tassel, and underneath the tassel and extending to the bottom of the placard, in large red Chinese characters, is a notice of Christian preaching. To the left of the notice, in black, are given the time and places of the meetings; to the right, also in black, is an invitation that may be rendered thus: "How did you come into this world? Why were you born unto it? When you die where are you going? All who want to hear the answer come to the meetings. We will tell you very simply. Young and old, men and women, come and welcome. We will show you how to serve God and how to serve man."

Besides posting these placards, invitations printed on thin red paper are scattered far and wide. One of these, of which more than a hundred thousand copies have been distributed, may be rendered thus: "There is no one in the world who does not desire happiness, but how will you find it? There is no one who would not rather do right than do wrong, but how is that possible? Death comes to all; are you ready to die? What is the path that man should walk? How can one gain true happiness? What teaching will give you peace of mind? Only Christianity the gift of the true God."

In addition to these particulars should be mentioned house-to-house visitation, in which the attempt is made to extend to all in the neighbourhood an invitation. One pastor, through the members of his congregation, sent out some three hundred personal invitations to persons who were known to have more or less knowledge of Christianity; a plan which produced excellent results. There is also street preaching. But to mention only one thing more in this connection; processions pass along the streets, headed by banners of white cloth, some eighteen inches wide by six or eight feet long. On the lower part of the banner is written in large characters, Kirisuto Kyo Taikyo

36

Dendo; on the upper part is a red Greek or Roman cross. All this in a city where thirty years ago, notice-boards were set up declaring Christianity a capital crime, and in whose public museum to-day are exhibited the brass plates with raised figures of Christ on the cross, worn almost smooth by the feet of those who were required to stamp on them as a test that they were not Christians.

The public meetings in the evenings, which are usually preceded by meetings for children, begin at half-past seven. The churches are filled. In some cases people go away because there is no more room, a thing that has not been seen for twelve or fifteen years. In the old days not infrequently there was more or less of disorder; with scarcely an exception those who now come listen respectfully and attentively. The character of the preaching is evangelical, but not of any one particular type. God is our father, Christ is a divine Saviour, man is a sinner, sin is debt, bondage, death; Christianity offers atonement, forgiveness, a new life; man should repent, should confide in Christ, should go to God in prayer. One preacher lays emphasis on one truth, another on another. Nor can it be said that any one truth, or any one way of presenting truth, is preëminently effective. There is no excitement, a fact that has been referred to by many with satisfaction. On the other hand, an observing and thoughtful Japanese pastor expressed to me the opinion that the absence of deep feeling may be in part at least due to the fact that the preaching is not in a marked degree what used to be described as searching.

The methods followed in conducting the meetings are the ones familiar to those who have attended similar meetings at home. At the close of the preaching any who may be willing to express the desire to become Christians are asked to raise a hand or to stand. Sometimes there is no response, though usually there is; and when once the rising begins, it commonly goes on until a considerable number have risen. Those who have risen, and any others who are willing to do so, are then invited to form themselves into groups for private conversation; the men and the women being conducted to different parts of the room. Into the opposite galleries, if the church is one with galleries. Each one of these groups is assigned to a leader, who speaks to the members personally, endeavors to remove difficulties, to give necessary instruction, and to deepen any impression already received. He also urges all to attend regularly the meetings now going on and takes their names and addresses in order that the church may keep in touch with them. During this time of conversation the body of Christians who are not so engaged gather in front of the pulpit for prayer. In this men and women alike take part; sometimes two or three praying at the same time. There is however no disorder. The meeting usually closes between nine and ten o'clock.

Besides these evening meetings there is held in each district of the city in which special work is being carried on, a daily afternoon prayer meeting, and those who are engaged in the work or are interested in it assemble together. These meetings are well attended; frequently from two hundred and fifty to three hundred persons are present. They are regarded by all as among the essentials. Besides the more strictly religious exercises, among which prayer is prominent, a brief report from each church in the district is presented. This report always includes the number of new inquirers. The entire number of inquirers thus reported in Tokyo and Yokohama must now amount to nearly or quite 4,000.

You will observe that I speak of *inquirers*. Frequently they are described as converts, or as those who have confessed Christ, or as Christians. In the case of some of them, no doubt, and in that of many of them, it is believed, these expressions are correct descriptions; but in speaking of them as a class, inquirers is the right word. How many are seeking after God as men seek for hidden treasure the future only will reveal. Regarding the percentage of those who are promising there is naturally some difference of opinion, but the general feeling now is one of hopefulness.

Do the inquirers as a rule know anything about Christianity? This question I have asked repeatedly, and the common answers amount to this:—

There are three classes. Many know practically nothing about it beyond the name; a considerable number have a general knowledge of it; some know a good deal about it. This knowledge has come from the general spread of Christian ideas through the introduction of foreign literature, the press, and contact in various ways with Christian civilization; from the dissemination of distinctly Christian literature in Japan; from the influence direct and indirect of Christian schools; from intercourse with Christian relatives or friends; from occasional listening to Christian lectures or attendance at Christian services. The pastor who sent out the three hundred invitations told me that a considerable number of his inquirers had for some time attended his church irregularly. Another told me that one young man said to him: "My parents were Christians, and when I was a child I was baptized." These are spoken of as cases to some degree typical. By common consent the questions asked by the inquirers as a class to-day are far less crude, and the knowledge of Christianity possessed by them far greater than was the case with those of fifteen years ago.

What is to be done for the inquirers in order to gather them into the Church and make them worthy members of it? This is the question which all are asking.

One encouraging fact is that in so many cases the inquirers live in the vicinity of the church where they are enrolled. One pastor stated that there was not a block in the neighborhood of his church in which there was not at least one of those on his list, and that in one block there were sixteen. This of course brings a large percentage locally within easy reach. In some churches social meetings have already been held in order that the church members may make the acquaintance of the inquirers. Most of the inquirers are employed during the day, including of course Sundays, and therefore for the present at least there must be meetings for them in the evening. The minds of a number are turning towards the establishment of a systematic course of catechetical instruction and in some churches such classes for catechumens have already been organized. All feel that in the instruction and care of the inquirers lie the chief hopes and chief difficulties of the movement.

How is this sudden change in the condition of affairs to be accounted for? I think that the first answer that nine Japanese Christians out of ten would give to this question would be, "It is an answer to prayer." On inquiring of them regarding secondary causes I have received the following replies: (1) There has been a revival of Christian fellowship among the ministers of the Churches. (2) There is a widespread moral unrest, a general feeling that ethically Japan is not what it was; a belief that new moral forces are needed, that they cannot be had apart from religion, that Christianity is the only religion worthy of consideration, and that it should be looked into. (3) The notification issued by the government some two years ago, which indirectly gave to Christianity legal recognition, has removed from the minds of many of the more ignorant a vague remaining fear of harm of some kind, and from those of many of the more intelligent a similar fear of social or official injury. (4) Especially (what has already been referred to) the gradual growth of a class outside of the Church composed of those who know something of Christianity and are more or less favorably disposed to it; a class of men and women in some respects strikingly like those in the Roman empire who had come directly or indirectly under the influence of the synagogue, and in whom the Apostles found a field specially prepared to receive the seed of the gospel.

In conclusion it should be said that much that I have written is rather a record of current opinion than of ascertained fact; and that all is written before it is possible to forecast the future with anything like confidence.

MR. MACNAIR:—"The matters of interest to the Council with which I have been personally connected during the past year are (1) the work of the Promoting Committee on inter-mission comity and co-operation; and (2) the preparation of a hundred or more hymns for the use of all the Protestant Christians in Japan, and of a hymnal for the joint use of several of the Churches, our own included. The Promoting Committee report* is in your hands, and I have nothing to say further regarding it than that there is every prospect of its meeting with the approval of the requisite number of the missionaries to permit of the early organization of the proposed Standing Committee.† Work has progressed favorably on the Uniform Hymns also. There will be 125 hymns in all, and they should be completed by the end of the summer or in the early autumn.† I am glad to report concerning the joint hymnal project, which was discussed at the time of the General Conference last fall, that while at first a union of only three of the Churches seemed practicable—our own, the Baptist and the Congregational—there is now good reason to expect the coöperation of the Methodists as well, and of practically all but the Episcopalians.† The preparation of the book will take considerable time, a year or more; but the union will be worth the delay.

You doubtless have in hand printed information concerning the Taikyo Dendo movement as carried on in Tokyo during the last six or eight weeks. The awakening is a very remarkable one, and has

---

* See Appendix I.
† These expectations have since been realized.

already had substantial results in the shape of additions to the churches. There are large classes of inquirers, one in Shiba for example, where night after night from 100 to 150 men gather for the serious study of Christianity. It has been very inspiring to see people assemble again and again in such numbers as to necessitate the closing of church doors to prevent over-crowding, and then to have them remain by the score for further inquiry and instruction.

My regular personal work is the same as formerly—preaching in Tokyo and at various points in the neighboring province of Chiba. A good deal of my time is taken up, however, with the revision and consolidation of the hymn-books, the work to which I have just referred. I am secretary of the committee and have the general direction of the revision movement."

Mr. HAWORTH:—Mr. Haworth was transferred to the East Japan Mission in the fall of 1820, and reports his work as supplying vacant pulpits here and there, taking part in the Synod's special evangelistic work in the Tokyo Yokohama district, in Shimotsuke and Hitachi, and in the Nagoya region; also in the Committee work and preaching in connection with the Twentieth Century Evangelistic work of the Evangelical Alliance. He has had the oversight of three churches; two of which have now been placed under the Mission Board of the Nippon Kirisuto Kyokwai, the mission making its grant through the Board instead of directly to the churches. It is hoped that thus better results will be obtained. Mr. Haworth suggests that the Council take into consideration the advisibility of raising the salaries of pastors and evangelists; and also recommends the sending of representative men to America or Europe for extended study. He adds, "The most significant work in Japan at the present time, it seems to me, is the increasing tendency towards unity in practical service. The present developments in connection with the Tuikyo Dendo in Tokyo show what can be done when Christians forget their denominational limits and come together for service. The movement for union among the Methodist Churches and missions and the endeavors after a corporate oneness as suggested by the Conference last year, are refreshing signs of the deepening hold of the Spirit of Christ upon the hearts of his children in Japan."

Mr. LANDIS:—"Recently in connection with the renewed religious interest in Tokyo a number of our students are coming forth; twenty-eight are to be baptized to-morrow (June 22) and more will follow we trust in the near future. A part of my work has to do with the Sunday-school Helps; the Teacher's Monthly falling to my lot to edit for half the year: Dr. Albrecht having taken the other half. As I write a large part of it, this form a pretty arduous piece of work. This year too the editing and proof reading of the Tokyo Conference Report falls to my lot. The amount of work entailed by this report, especially the getting together and editing of the Appendix, few will appreciate when done; and the less so because of the great delay. I have also a weekly Bible class connected with the Shiba Church S. S. Also a monthly service with the young men in Yokohama connected with the work of Miss

40

Case of our mission there. The above with a variety of architectural and other work keeps me out of mischief elsewhere, though occasionaly I have a chance to preach in various places. The remarkable work recently beginning in Tokyo and Yokohama will no doubt be more fully reported to you by others the nature of whose work brings them in closer connection therewith. The work has been heartily participated in by our men and our churches. And already an abundant harvest is in sight which however we trust is but an earnest of what is yet to be; inaugurating in fact a more extensive work of God's spirit, we trust, then Japan has seen hitherto."

MISS YOUNGMAN:—"I am still carrying on my two missions in Tokyo and one in Kamakura. These are always open from seven in the morning until ten at night; an evangelist, who is the Superintendent, being always present. A reading room, daily prayer meeting, children's meetings, women's meetings, Sunday-schools, and preaching every night are the channels through which we hope to reach people with the gospel. The Ueno Mission has a service every Sabbath at two o'clock in the Ueno Park. This is the eleventh year of these missions. I have had orphan children in my family for nine years. For seven years I have assisted the Kozen Sha in its work for lepers at Megoro. The rescue work has also been one in which I have been much interested. The Leper Home has been greatly blessed of God both temporally, and spiritually. There are 41 inmates; and although none can be said to have gone out cured, many have gone from us much improved; and out of 41 inmates thirty are Christians. During the year we have built a chapel, to the delight of the patients, and especially those of us who go there regularly for religious teaching. We have also increased our grounds by one thousand *tsubo* during the past year. Of all the different kinds of work which it has been my privilege to do in Japan, this bringing comfort and rest to the bodies, and salvation to the souls of these poor afflicted ones seems the most blessed. As my mission seems to be to sow the seed by *all* waters, results will be hard to report and must be left to the great harvest day when if the sheaves are found lying at the Master's feet, it will matter little who was the instrument used in bringing them. I have not looked up statistics but Ueno has reached about 25000, Kamejima 13.000, and Kamakura 3000. There have been several baptized in various churches brought in through the missions. Missionaries of various denominations have assisted in the work and we bless God for what he has wrought."

MRS. MCCAULEY:—"The work under my charge during the year has been as follows: Two Primary Schools, registered as Kakushi Gakko. They have the Ordinary and Higher Primary School courses of study; and our pupils are allowed to enter other schools on the diploma we give without question. We have full religious privileges. We have enrolled in one, 120; in the other, 88 pupils. A Sunday-school is well attended. A normal class for the study of the Sunday-school lesson is held weekly at which all the teachers attend; also a weekly teachers prayer meeting. Work is done in the Charity Hospital where from time to time souls are brought into a new life

41

and many after leaving the hospital become regular attendants at the worship in the churches. Tracts and leaflets have been scattered far and wide. The life of the teachers has been faithful, earnest, zealous in every case. So that we have much cause for thankfulness."

Mrs. MacNair and Miss West:—" There have been fifteen students in the Training School for Bible-women this year. Almost without exception these have been earnest, faithful, purposeful women. Owing to financial limitations, the practical direct evangelistic work of the school has been much restricted. Fewer Sunday-schools and meetings for the instruction of women and children have been carried on and fewer country stations occupied in summer work than formerly. But despite these discouragements the year has been one of blessing and profit not only to its own students and teachers, but also, we have reason to hope, to many who have been brought within the sphere of its influence.

Seven students did effective and acceptable work in four country stations during the summer months. Four* of the graduates of the school have been employed as Bible-women. One in the Kisarazu and Yokota stations in Chiba province, one in connection with the kindergarten in Shinagawa and two in general city work. These women have been faithful and diligent in giving systematic instruction in Bible truth to many of their country-women who are debarred by domestic, social or other considerations from the opportunities open to men. They have engaged in Sunday-school work and in conducting and assisting in women's meetings. They also, together with the students of the Training School, took an active part in the Taikyo Dendo movement.

The Kindergarten, reopened in Shinagawa in April 1900 with the distinctly granted privilege of declaring its Christian character, has kept up its full quota (limited by government regulation) of pupils during the year. From forty to fifty names have been on the monthly rolls and good work has been done in some of the homes from which the little ones come.

The regular semi-weekly visitation of several years past in one of the city hospitals has been continued; and it is hoped and believed that more than one soul has been helped in preparation to meet its God, and that some have gone down into the Dark Valley calmly trusting in salvation through the One Name. In this work thousands of carefully selected tracts and portions of Scripture have been distributed. These have been eagerly read by not only the invalids but also the friends and relatives in attendance; and the time of one Bible-woman has been occupied for the most part in taking advantage of the openings thus offered by visiting and instructing convalescents and their friends in their homes."

Miss Sarah Gardner:—" In its general features the history of the Joshi Gakuin for the past year does not differ essentially from that of other years. During the absence of Miss Milliken on furlough the school has had the advantage of the services of Mrs. Davidson of the

* Reduced by cut from six.

Scotch Mission, and of Miss Norman of the Canada Methodist Church. The number of pupils is now somewhat more than two hundred. The work has gone on much as usual.

But in one particular the year has been one long to be remembered. From beginning to end it has seemed to be a quiet harvest time—a time of reaping after much sowing. Many of the Christian girls have been greatly quickened spiritually, and from among the rest fifty-six believe that they have received Christ as their Saviour. Of the one hundred boarding pupils all of the older girls are now Christians. The recent evangelistic movement was influential in bringing some eighteen of the girls to a decision; but there has been a clear manifestation of the presence of the Holy Spirit from the beginning of the school year. With thankful hearts we praise God for what he has wrought."

MISS CASE:—"There are certain times when overwhelmed with sorrow, we cannot give utterance to our deepest emotion. We prefer to sit in quietness, and hear what the Lord our God would say. This explains why there was no report last summer. Only those who had started new work in a new place could sympathize with us as we opened our Industrial School for Ladies one year ago last April. However, in September, we entertained hopes of success, as there were several additions, making the number of pupils enrolled 22. The Rev. Mr. Yamamoto acts as principal. Besides giving half an hour every morning to Christian teaching, he had the usual Japanese secular branches. Music and English, as well as sewing, etiquette, and the arrangement of flowers, are taught. An English class of eleven young men has been formed for the purpose of increasing the attendance and interest of the Sunday Bible class. These students sing several songs every morning after which a verse of Scripture is explained, and the usual English lesson proceeds. Much Christian work is being accomplished by a cooking class under English methods, which was formed at the beginning of April. This class has been the means of gathering in ladies occupying positions of influence. The usual visits among Sunday-school pupils, delinquent church members and the sick have been made. Only the warmest of hospitality was shown even in the homes of the non-Christians. Meetings for the Y. M. C. A., prayer and preaching services, women's monthly meetings, and the pastors' weekly inquiry meeting, are held in our day school building. On the third Sabbath of each month Mr. Landis, of the Meiji Gakuin, gives a Christian lecture to the young men in the same building. These lectures have helped to stimulate the younger Christians, and have caused others to understand more of faith and the love of God. The Sabbath Bible class for male adults numbers twenty-nine, twenty being the average present on each Sabbath. Peloubet's Notes have been the means of helping some of the young men to receive Christ, while to others, they have given a clearer knowledge of the Bible. Two members of the class were baptized during the year, and eight more are being prepared for baptism. The spiritual condition of the church is better than ever before. At the next communion, over thirty hope to be admitted to the Lord's table for the first time. The Sunday-school has an attendance of seventy-five pupils. The Honako Sunday-school is in a flourishing condition.

Every Monday morning, a preaching Service is conducted at the establishment of the Fukuin Printing Company, for the one hundred and forty men and women there. Tracts and Christian papers are regularly distributed. The two faithful Bible women continue their weekly round of duties."

MR. PIERSON:—"Mrs. Pierson and I came to this new city last summer. Our work has been distinctly evangelistic. There is enough here in the city itself to occupy our full time. Asahigawa is about ten years old. Population about 15,000. There are great barracks near by with a soldier population of some thousands increasing every year. There are large and small farms in every direction until you come to the mountains many miles off on the east and not so far on the other side. There are three railroads running north, south and east from this place. Railroad shops too, ultimately to have over 1000 workmen. Besides there are three soldier colonies lying out toward the east. So we have plenty of work. People come singly and in groups: carpenters, children, Ainu people, soldiers et al.

The people are most accessible. There is little opposition except hurry and money. We do not find it at all necessary to teach English. People often come to be taught. We almost invariably decline. We have neither the time nor strength, we say. Evangelistic work is so inviting and so possible that it seems to me positively wrong to use the time to teach English. We did think of adopting the line of work pursued by Mr. Brokaw in Hiroshima; but we find we do not need to advertise. Semi Kyudosha (inquirers) are already plentiful. We do however quite a little work by mail. From Nov. to March advertising would be a good method here I think.

Ainu come to us now and then. There are quite a number near by: Working for them is interesting. They show their whole hearts. The C. M. S. has done the great work for them and are doing it. We feel even in thus incidently touching it as though we were encroaching on others' territory. All honor to Mr. Batchelor. It is sad to see the men going to ruin under excessive drinking. They have little else in the way of comfort. Hardly any education. A young man here yesterday bright and ambitious could barely read the katakana. But they have not lack of mental power. Mrs. Pierson has done quite a little work for the Ainu women. Seven have signed the temperance pledge. A large number have attended the Kyofu Kwai recently.

The people would be glad to have a high school for girls here. The Meiji Jo Gakko (was) to start a branch. I have been asked if I would teach in a private Chu Gakko if it were started; but we feel that these means are too indirect when short roads lie open all around the compass.

Ours is the usual life of a country missionary intensified perhaps by the busy and free life about us, and opportunities that the people themselves, and the government with its roads and railroads are constantly making. Last year we offered to our believers here two rooms in our lower floor as a preaching place. But they raised over three hundred yen; which, combined with funds on hand for some years and others recently subscribed purchased a plot of ground near the

44

railroad shops and built a 400 *yen* church; not to mention the repairing of a house that came with the property as a Pastor's home. We are holding well attended gospel meetings there now, to our great delight and with thanksgiving. One believer gave 100 *yen*; another 50 *yen* (accumulated at the rate of 10 *sen* per day from his earnings); and another, 50 *yen*. An inquirer gave 100 *yen* worth of land.

We are doing some tract and visiting work and find it most interesting. You discover believers and inquirers. This being a new place many people of Christian connection are continually coming in; but some such work as this seems necessary to find them out. Bible selling I have done something at; but not very much lately. There was some objection on the part of the government railroad but that is removed.

I want to report for a church that seemed wounded and of little life. The evangelist at Mombetsu a man of faith and faithfulness, a man of prayer and belief in the Holy Spirit's help, has done good work against wind and snow, physical and spiritual, and the church is living and growing.

We hope for a Hokkaido Presbytery some day. We have three self-sustaining churches here already: *i.e.* at Hakodate, Sapporo, and the Seien Kyokwai at Takeichi-no-Jo. A quiet growth and unity both in itself and with other churches in that city. At Mororan there have been only a few baptisms. We regret that two of the Christians do not close shops on Sunday. Until that is done I do not hope for much growth. At Takigawa Buddhist influence is strong, and there is opposition to the present special evangelistic movement. However there is growth in grace and establishment in the faith. The Hokkaido is very earnest in the *Taikyo Dendo*.

The Sapporo Girls School has been reinforced by the efficient services of Miss Wells; the number of girls entering has greatly increased and a work of the spirit has been manifested."

Miss Rose:—"The Sei Shin Jo Gakko of Otaru graduated its first class this spring. Both of the graduates are Christians and are now employed in the school as assistant teachers. Three were graduated from the Primary Department at the same time. Of these one is a Christian. Two of them will remain to complete the advanced course. Including the kindergarten department about 130 pupils have been in attendance during the year. An increase of 40 over last report. Of this number however, only about one-third are in attendance during the months of the deepest snow. We have also a number of Sunday-schools in charge and a weekly adult Bible class."

2. West Japan Mission of the Presbyterian Church in the U.S.A. (Northern).

STATION	POPULATION	FU OR KEN	POPULATION
Kyoto	351461	Kyoto Fu	990762
Osaka	811855	Osaka „	1.591221
Hiroshima	114231	Aki Ken	1.436647
Yamaguchi	17387	Yamaguchi Ken	975319
Matsuyama	74728	Ehime „	992552
Fukui	43929 } Ishikawa „	745556
Kanazawa	81520 }		

Dr. Alexander:—The Kyoto Church has made slow but steady progress during the year notwithstanding the fact that it has been without a pastor all the while. The number on the roll is now greater than ever before, and attendance on the stated services of the church is regular and good. The want of a pastor so keenly felt for a year past is now happily supplied by the coming of Mr. Otani who is under the care of the Board of Home Missions of the Church of Christ in Japan from which the church will in receive aid for the time being. No aid has been granted from the mission since May 1900. For some months past the attendance on the evening services has been materially increased, owing to the fact that the resident missionary has given a thirty minutes talk in English before the beginning of the regular preaching service. By this means a number of young men have been induced to attend and to remain for the sermon in Japanese after the English talk is over. Evangelistic work outside the church has been carried on under difficulties but not without tokens of success. This branch of the work suffered a great loss in the death of Mr. Ishibashi Shigenori in November last. As an Evangelist Mr. Ishibashi was earnest and faithful, and his loss is deeply felt. It is gratifying however to know that his death was triumphant, and that he left us in the assurance that he was being graciously called of the Heavenly Father to higher service and greater fulness of blessing.

Evangelistic work in Tsuruga and Obama has had to be given up owing to the cut in our appropriations. The work in the kindergartens of which there are two in the city has continued, and was never more prosperous than at the present. The homes of the children are open to visits from Christian teachers, and the children themselves attend the Sunday-schools. The Sunday-schools are therefore full, and they are well conducted. Kyoto is a conservative old city and responds but slowly and indifferently to progressive influences from the outside; but the outlook is not wanting in signs of improvement, and we have reason to thank God and take courage."

Mr. Jones: — "Really there seems to be a perceptable moving among the dry bones in this valley of Buddhism. No rush to Christianity of course, but more of a willingness to know something about it. Inquirers are more numerous, audiences larger, interest deeper, and at least five are now ready to receive baptism. To this number should perhaps be added another, an old lady of a prominent family. Three of these have very bitter spiritual foes in those of their own households. Mention is to be made of two who were to have been baptized at the close of last year. The spirit of inquiry is manifestly in the ascendant. Responding to advertisements in the local papers, requests for Christian literature have come from many widely scattered villages. Considering the grip idolatry has here a surprisingly large number of copies of the Scriptures have been sold by both the book stores and the evangelists. During the three hundredth anniversary of the founding of the city, in three days we sold Scriptures and other Christian literature to the amount of about 17 yen. The tracts were sold at a nominal price, about one-fourth the list price. Our little eight paged Yako devoted to Bible study has now a semi-monthly circulation of 900. More than half of these we send out direct to those who have notified us of their desire to investigate Christianity. The remainder are subscribed for by missionaries for similar use in their own fields. With the beginning of the year the Rev. G. W. Fulton of Kanazawa kindly consented to prepare an exposition of the Gospel of Luke. About half of the paper is used for the exposition of the Scripture text and the remainder for enforcement by illustration, etc. of the main teaching in the portion dealt with. Regular weekly meetings for women and children have been held in Fukui and four outside places. In addition to the regular meetings, the magic lantern with views from the life of Christ has been helpful. One of the converts, the wife of a railroad official, Mrs. Jones says, is the most remarkable seeker she has met with in all Japan. Another feature of our work that promises good results, is teaching a class of government school students to sing Christian hymns in Japanese. Beside our regular weekly meetings for men in two of our outstations and less frequent visits to three others, we have various Bible classes which are encouraging. Students on being unable to persuade us to teach English, instead of going away offended, have been led to study Christianity."

Mr. Dunlop:—"The staff at Kanazawa during the past year has been the Rev. and Mrs. G W. Fulton, and the Rev. and Mrs. J. G. Dunlop, in evangelistic work; Miss Shaw in the Hoku Riku Jo Gakko; and Miss Luther in the Shirtsu Eiwa Gakko. Miss Glenn, of the Hoku Riku Jo Gakko, has been absent from the station all the year through illness. The evangelistic work in the City of Kanazawa is largely in the hands of the two churches. The missionaries work in connection with the churches, and besides conduct one preaching place, and have just built another, which they are about to open. The preaching place work this year, as in the past, has been altogether seed-sowing. Large audiences gather in favorable weather, but no visible results occur from the preaching. The outstations are Dai Shoji, Komatsu, and Koyama. In all of these there has been some progress. There have been no baptisms, but the audiences are larger, and there are unwonted toleration and interest. One evangelist is stationed at Dai Shoji, and one at Toyama; and these travel widely in the surrounding country, visiting inquirers and holding meetings when

47

they have opportunity. Mr. Fulton has also come in touch with several hundred country inquirers by means of his correspondence Bible Study. This is a work with great possibilities. It is a new enterprise in Kanazawa. This year, another new enterprise which promises well is the selling of scriptures and tracts at the religions festivals, both in Kanazawa and in the surrounding towns. The larger church at Kanazawa celebrated its twentieth anniversary on June 1st. Mr. Winn, the father of the church, was present to take part in the anniversary services The church has had a successful year. There have been over twenty baptisms. Many special evangelistic meetings have been held during the winter and spring, to commemorate the new century and this twentieth church anniversary. The smaller church is in a weak state, though here too there is some improvement noticeable. Altogether the outlook in Kanazawa is more promising than ever before."

MISS LUTHER:—"The past year has been full of startling events to all interested in missions, for the eyes of the world have been turned toward China, as the heroes of the faith in that land have stood persecution and have borne even death for the cause of Christ. Although no such startling events have taken place in our field of labor, the year has not been without its shadows. When the report for the school was sent in last year, two ladies were regularly engaged in the work; but the shadow of sickness entered our midst, and Miss Glenn has been laid aside all the year, while Miss Shaw has several times been compelled to stop work on account of illness. This irregularity of teachers in the English department, and also other necessary work have been met as well as possible with stranded friends from China. So China's loss was our temporary gain.

There have been forty-five pupils enrolled during the year. Of this number twenty are baptized Christians. While seven others, although giving every evidence of faith, have not been allowed baptism by parents or guardians. The C. E. Society has earnestly carried on its work. Twenty-eight of the girls are members, while all of them attend its meetings. Their endeavors for Christ have been of a very practical nature. After a disastrous fire at Takeoka they sent five yen to assist in caring for the destitute, and received recognition for the gift from the Governor himself. By making and selling knitted articles quite a sum was on hand to be given to the poor at Christmas. This they used with discretion and cheered lonely hearts. The Society also contributes monthly to the Florence Critenden Home in Tokyo.

A year ago the leaders of the Young Womans Temperance Society endeavored to obtain permission to prohibit public dancing in the Park during the annual soldiers' festival. They failed last year, but with the aid of other societies in the city this year they obtained their request. Although on the day of the festival when the societies took charge of a tea booth none of the Y. W. T. S. were present; it not being thought wise. The results accomplished were largely through their efforts and prayers. Twenty-six of the girls belong to this society. A large proportion of the students come from the surrounding towns and villages. Of these only twelve have

Christian homes. Eight teach regularly in the various Sunday-schools. In March six graduated from the Japanese Department. Of this number four have remained to complete the English course.

As this department only occupies the afternoon they are all regularly employed during the morning. One is in charge of some school work; another assists in the mission kindergarten; while two are teaching in a *joshikwai* recently opened in one of the preaching places. As a thank offering for Miss Shaw's recovery from a severe illness last fall. her home church and friends sent a sum of money sufficient to build a chapel from material bought from a former boys school in this city. This building which is now being put up will make a valuable addition to the school property and also be a place where public meetings can be held from time to time. Although much anxiety for sick ones has been felt, and many changes in order to suit work to new helpers have had to be made, all have been courageous, have prayed more earnestly, trusted more implicitly and received quietly what the Master saw best to send. He has abundantly blessed and will continue to bless this work for girls in Kanazawa.

When the Kanazawa Childrens School opened in April, 1900, there were fifty-nine children enrolled in the primary department, and 28 in the kindergarten. Within a month after opening, we were called upon to say goodbye to the one who had started, and who has had charge of the school for so many years, Miss Porter who returned to America on furlough. The work of the year has been much the same as in the past. During the spring months, the attendance increased so rapidly, especially in the kindergarten department, that we were compelled to build a new room, which, added to the former room, is now at the close of the year almost too small for the number of children on the roll, not to mention those wishing to enter. The religious life of the school has been encouraging The children have actively worked in their junior society, and also their Temperance Society; while, with their money earned from their knitting society, they have contributed *yen* 5 to the Okayama, and *yen* 5 to the Nohe, Orphanages. Special exercises on Childrens' Day, Christmas and Easter, brought out many of the day school pupils, who do not regularly attend the Sunday-school. We find this special preparation for these days a good inducement to more interest in the Sunday-school.

In March we had our annual commencement exercises, when seven graduated from the kindergarten, five of whom entered the regular school. We had no regular class of graduates from the primary school this year; so we opened in April with all of our old scholars, and a new class of fourteen. The attendance now numbering 103 in the two departments, 40 of whom are in the kindergarten.

We have had a good deal of trouble because of sick teachers during the past year. Substitutes were hard to find, and changes were bad for the school. The horizon seemed bright and clear for a few weeks, and we were looking forward to a successful year. Then a shock came, which was indeed a shock to all concerned. The authorities refused to grant the fourteen new scholars, who entered the first year's class, the necessary permission to remain in a private school, the excuse being 'religion is bad for children.' The necessary officials were all interviewed the Governor finally promising to settle the difficulty. We

49

breathed a little easier, but only for a short time. Again they refused ; this time, they say 'there is no need of private schools'. In the meantime several parents have put their children in other schools. We do not know how it will be settled, we believe as He has cared for the work in the past, He will continue to care for it now. So we hope the shadows will soon pass away, and the horizon become bright and clear again."

Mr. Winn:—" There has been nothing very unusual in the nature of the work in this place. A little kindergarten at Sakai is the only school that we are immediately connected with. That has had from fifteen to twenty-five children in attendance during the year, and has had some influence in helping on the Sabbath-school which was maintained at the preaching place. Then work in connection with that preaching place has been, to a good degree, successful; and would have been much more so, had there not arisen discontent in the minds of a few Christians with the preacher stationed there. That trouble grew, until a special committee of Presbytery was asked to settle matters. The preacher has gone elsewhere, and the future of the work at Sakai is uncertain.

The mission supports two preaching places in this city, where various meetings are held for sowing the seed of the gospel. At one there are a flourishing Sunday-school and a Woman's meeting, beside the preaching and work for young men. At the other, many hear the word preached, and an effort to reach young men is made with some success. The two churches, which have grown from the work of our mission, have not made any great advance. The South Church has received a large number of additions; over thirty since January of this year; but I have not seen any special awakening to new life or zeal. The Sabbath evening attendance is better of late ; the evening congregations run from 50 or more at times. The North Church has also had additions, and its audiences are larger than a year or two ago. The South Church has recently raised its pastor's salary to *yen* twenty-five per month, and a parsonage. The contributions of these churches have amounted to considerably over *yen* 700.

My comtry work has been in *statu quo* for I have had no evangelist to aid me in it. At one place I took a few New Testaments and Gospels to the leading bookstore. The merchant was glad to put them on sale, and the next time I went there they had nearly all been sold. He will take more, and probably a constant sale will be established for the Scriptures in that town.

The churches and pastors have taken part in the Taikyo Dendo; meetings have been held in connection with that forward movement ; but the results, so far as I know, have been small. Unless the increased attendance mentioned may be connected with it.

The night classes for English and Bible teaching have been successful in arousing interest among the young men of the North Church. It has led some into church membership. I am led constantly to lament the little that seems to be accomplished : the fewness of those who are receiving and obeying the gospel.

P. S. Since writing my report the Osaka churches have shared in a measure in an awakening like the one in Tokyo. All the churches have a larger or smaller number of inquirers connected with each of them. Our North and South Churches have together 70 or 80. I understand that the same kind of meetings will be resumed in the fall. I have great hopes that even larger results will be seen than have already appeared. I see no reason why this expectation may not be fulfilled. Prayer and effort on the part of God's people will surely be blessed of God when engaged in with real desire to glorify him."

Miss Garvin:—"June 26th closed a good year for us here. The requirements for both entrance and graduation have been raised one year; and this without any falling off in numbers. But thus raising the grade of scholarship has raised already the standing and influence of the school. We have held our own numerically in face of the fact that the finest High School for girls in the city has just been opened a few blocks from us with buildings and equipments of the best. Our total enrolment is eighty-four with an average attendance of fifty-six. The boarding department has increased from ten to twenty-six. Some of our pupils have come from as far away as Kyushin, showing that the school is extending its influence over a larger territory year by year. With great enthusiasm the graduates met last year to form an Alumnae Association.

As they scattered to their homes again after a feast and a good time generally, it was with a warmer feeling toward their Alma Mater and a determination to do all in their power to send pupils to us. Our teaching force has come to include four of the graduates and we are working toward a teaching force of Christian teachers only. But teachers able to teach the higher branches are not within the reach of a mission school teacher's fund. We have all Christian teachers now except three. Our head teacher Mr. Aoyama continues his efficient work and strong Christian influence among us. Without him it would be impossible to report such progress among us intellectually.

But it is along spiritual lines we feel that our progress has been greatest. Since Mr. Aoyama's advent we have held regular chapel service on Sunday afternoon, and prayer meeting on Friday evening. Many of the day pupils come in to these meetings; some of them are hindered by their parents from attending a Christian church, but this service is permissible even to them.

The Bible classes have been carried on as usual the first lesson in the morning systematically and consecutively. The girls have been having training in Christian work in two ways. The Sunday-school is under the care of the Christian girls under our supervision. But best of all our Christian Endeavor Society not yet a year old has proved itself a normal and healthy infant by remarkable growth and activity. At the time of organization we had forty-four members, fourteen of whom were active. We now have fifty-seven with thirty-two active. Our active membership, Christians who take the full pledge of the C. E. Society, has increased more than 100%. The associate membership has decreased, a number of the associate members having gone over into the active membership. The parents all approve of this society among the girls, and parents who will not permit their daughters to be baptized do not object to this. We have found it a means of great growth in a Christian training school unequalled by any effort hitherto

51

made in the way of preparation for definite Christian work. The girls feel the responsibility of it. They learn how to lead a meeting; how to prepare for the same; how to make a stranger welcome; how to get a young Christian started to work; how to testify before an audience; how to give of their substance, et cetera. Gifts this year from the society amounted to sixteen yen. The number of Christians baptized during the year was twelve; and the number who entered the Church from the school fourteen."

Mr. Curtis:—" All our churches are making advance toward the goal of self-support. One church notably during the last calendar year contributed 207 yen. This contribution was made by 21 church members and was mostly for church repairs. The Taikyo Dendo has done good whenever it has touched. Christians have been stimulated and unbelievers reached in large numbers. An announcement of the last series of meetings was personally carried by the believers in Yamaguchi to every house in town with excellent results. The general attitude of the people in our entire field is favorable toward Christianity. Work among the educational classes is especially promising. Each of the five Middle Schools in the Ken has a Christian Teacher of English. Four of these young men have come out under the auspices of the Y. M. C. A. The fifth is a missionary. All are doing positive Christian work among the students. The completion of the Sanyo Railroad to Shimonoseki greatly facilitates the carrying on of our work in the Ken.
The Yamaguchi Girls School and Kindergarten are both in a flourishing condition; with 21 and 23 pupils respectively. Women's and mother's meetings conducted by the missionaries are well attended."

Miss Bigelow:—" The Kojo Jo Gakuin has made no special history this year; 33 pupils have been enrolled but at this writing only 23 are in attendance of whom three are Christians. These have been no baptisms during the year. This year the pupils are very young, the majority being of Koto Sho Gakko grade. More than half have been less than fifteen months in school. The school has taken nearly the entire time of Miss Biglow. Miss Palmer returned from her furlough in February to her residence in the Kojo Jo Gakuin, but her work is largely evangelistic."

Mr. Brokaw:—" Our efforts can be classified under five general heads: touring, house-to-house visitation, Sunday-school work, meetings and classes at home, and correspondence work. Taking the work as a whole, we are sorry to have to report that it has not been a year of ingathering. There have not been more than ten baptisms in the whole work, including the those in the church in Hiroshima. There has been no lack of inquirers; we can get good audiences anywhere, of which fact we have taken advantage to our utmost, but there are few who go any further than a general inquiry. The fact that few come out on the Lord's side is not due to open persecution, for there seems to be little; but the quiet undercurrent of public opinion rather causes many to hesitate. There is no denying the fact in our work that the current is against us.
Taking up the five heads of work briefly in their above order, we

have pushed the *touring* as it has never been done before. We have been enabled to do this more effectively than we had been able to do before, as a result of our correspondence and literature plan of which I will write later. Suffice it to say now that we have inquirers all over the *Ken* to whom we and our workers can go directly in our tours, and who also are willing to help us secure halls, theatres, etc., for lectures, preaching services, and magic lantern exhibitions. Two recent trips, one by myself and one by my colleague, will illustrate what we can do in this line. I was out a week, and held meetings of from 100 to 400 people in different towns every night. My colleague was out ten days, stayed two nights in most places, was in the mountain districts, where the towns have only a few thousand inhabitants, but was able to reach over two thousand people in the ten days.

In the matter of house-to-house visitation, our work is so inconspicuous that we had better pass over that head in silence. A natural inability along that line of work both on the part of the writer and his colleague, together with the unusually unsociable character of the people of this *Ken*, makes this work very difficult for us. The ladies of the station do the better work, but it is almost impossible to get into the homes. We are met at the door with a stony stare, and the stiffest sort of formal politeness, and an air of "so far thou shalt come and no farther."

In our Sunday-School work, we have been greatly hampered by the inability to secure rooms. The people want to rent, but when they hear of our purpose, they remark, "We cant rent for Yasu Kyo." In all the Sunday-schools which we have, there is a good and regular attendance. We have not tried any new or startling methods; but it is becoming a fixed conviction with me that we missionaries ought to do more work with the children. We must get hold of the children before they are filled with the false philosophies, misrepresentations, and prejudices of the schools and society at large. We have found the series of lessons prepared by Miss Deyo and for sale at the Keiseisha very valuable, and the workers praise it unstintedly. It makes the subject matter of our teaching orderly.

We have carried on a number of English and Japanese Bible classes at home, but we have not seen much result with the English. We refuse to teach the Bible in English, unless we are convinced that the pupil will understand what we say. The young men whom we teach undoubtedly understand, and whether the lack of results comes from the fact that they come more with a motive for studying English, or whether it comes from the general unfruitfulness of the present, I am not prepared to say.

Our greatest encouragement has come from our correspondence plan. The workers call it *Tsushin Dendo*, but the correspondence is only a part, and it might better be called Christian Literature Correspondence Work. We advertise in the local papers, by circulars after meetings, and by advertisements pasted in packages of tracts put in the R. R. stations, that we will send Christian books to any who wish to investigate Christianity. As the answers come in, we carefully record the address, give the applicant a number, and mark his number at his address on a map. We send out a special bundle of five or six tracts, and after the applicant has had time to read them, we send a letter asking

53

if there are any doubts, and whether he wishes to investigate farther, etc. On the basis of these replies, we send out new books, send personal letters, and when matters have developed sufficiently, prepare a tour, always by a Japanese worker first. The correspondents are looked up, and the real interest investigated. As the matter progresses, and requests come in from all over the province, we go out ourselves, hold public meetings with these correspondents acting as promoters, and also we meet these men ourselves. We have scattered hundreds of tracts in this way, have enabled our evangelists to go on their tours to some soul directly, and have opened up work in many new places where nothing has yet been done. There is no more of evangelists going out to some neighboring village, sitting around in a hotel, using up mission money, and sowing no seed. We make out the tours ourselves, and the men go with lists of places and names in their pockets, and are expected to report meeting the correspondent, his status, etc., or give some good reason, such as absence, why he was not met. The ones who are anxious for the light are thus discovered, and it is a pleasure to work where the Spirit also seems to be working. As a result of this plan, we have some real inquirers; some have received baptism both by us and by those of other Churches; others have been asking for baptism, and we can go to dozens of places, and find a way and a welcome, where it would have been hard to get any hold before.

This plan of work has compelled us to investigate the matter of tracts; which were the best, what were lacking, etc. My colleague has now in press a little catalogue, telling the correspondents where the Bible is purchaseable, describing Bibles, giving price and place of sale of the best tracts, and other information. I think this will be of value outside of our work. A great number of tracts had to be investigated, as we do not confine ourselves to only one of the Publishing and Societies.

In connection with the above plan, and to help the church here, we publish a little monthly paper called the Fukuin Geppo. This is sent to every one of the correspondents, and serves to keep up the interest. We also advertise the Fukui Yako in each package of tracts sent out, and have quite a list studying the Gospel of Luke through that medium. Messrs. Fulton of Kanazawa, Jones of Fukui, and Scudder of Nagano, are working this same Christian Literature Plan, and may have something to say about it. I understand that Mr. Fulton substitutes the Yako for our Geppo, and sends it to all correspondents.

The matter of self-support is in statu quo. Our mission made, and received permission from our Board for, a plan to pay to the Dendo Kyoku a sum of money each year for five years equal to the amount we are now paying to non-self-supporting churches. The idea was that the Dendo Kyoku was more able than we to bring churches up to their best in giving, and thus to self-support, while the mission would be free in five years. Such a plan might mean that some of the very weakest churches would be disbanded; but it is a question whether that is not wise any way, it seems to me. However for the present at least the plan has fallen through."

Mr. Doughty:—"I inclose you a portion of the last report made

54

to the mission on behalf of this station. It contains the new features of our work here. We are following along those lines with reasonable success. We have not advertised much more since that report was written but we now have some 325 names on our list of those studying with us in the country. Some of course have proved frauds, some have moved away, some have died, some are not very hopeful; but I am glad to add that several have been baptized and that others are applicants. We have honey-combed the Ken with Christian literature and have followed it up with long preaching tours extending to the limits of the Ken. By means of these inquirers we have been enabled to gain the attendance at these meetings of the most prominent people of the official class. In one case a doctor permitted the use of an empty ward of his hospital and in another a well-to-do farmer threw open his house for use as a meeting place. At one Chu Gakko in the interior of the Ken a class of 10 has been organized and two of them have asked for baptism. At another point in the Ken a Shinto priest in connection with the most scholarly man in the place is studying and teaching Christianity to a class of young men. At one village the principal man of the place and all the officials are studying Christianity. The head teacher and another teacher of the school of the same village are also studying. Of course it does not do to count too much on facts like these. It is one thing to study and another to repent, but it is surely a good and profitable thing to get so many in the heart of this Ken to even study the truth that alone has power to make them free. We continue to place literature in the railway stations though we bind the bundle more firmly than at first. One bundle will last for three or four months.

All the other work—church, Sunday-school and preaching place—goes on as usual."

Mr. Bryan :—"The chief thing to report with the work in connection with this young preaching place is the amount of personal work being done by the Christians and by those who have not yet received baptism. The attendance at the meetings has been steadily increasing for this reason. Not only do the inquirers attend the Sunday services, but the prayer meetings also. Inquirers as well as Christians take a deep interest in the work of the preaching place. The teaching of English by the evangelist has been one of the agencies by which the work here has prospered as well as it has. I came to Matsuyama only last fall so that the work in its plans and results reflects credit only on the evangelist and on those who are connected with the preaching place."

55

3. North Japan Mission of the Reformed (Dutch) Church in America.

STATION	POPULATION	FU OR KEN		POPULATION
Tokyo	1425366	Tokyo Fu		2075694
Yokohama	193762	Kanagawa Ken		916356
Nagano	30412	Nagano	,,	1262758
Morioka	32989	Iwate	,,	717895
Aomori	27991	Aomori	,,	611758

Dr. Wyckoff:—" Except for a little scattering work in other people's fields, and one Bible class in the Yotsuya preaching place in Tokyo, my whole work has been in connection with the Academic Department of the Meiji Gakuin. The conditions in the school have steadily improved during the year. The privilege of the postponement of conscription, which we had been obliged to give up because of the Instruction of 1899 forbidding religious exercises in all schools having government connection, was restored to us and we were recognized as being equivalent to a government Middle School. This alone caused an increase of pupils; but on May 7th 1901 new regulations for the admission of students to the government Higher Schools were published in the Official Gazette, and by the regulations our students have the same opportunity for entrance to the Higher Schools and the universities, that is given to graduates of the government schools of the same grade. This removes all troublesome disabilities, while at the same time we have all the religious services and teaching that we desire. This last change will probably not seriously effect the number of students for the present term, but we may expect a large increase in the autumn. At it is the number of pupils is larger than it has been for ten years. We have over one hundred and seventy-five enrolled and stragglers still coming in. We have already given notice that we will not receive any more pupils into the present higher classes of the Middle School course as that class is as large as we can conveniently care for ; besides we wish to discourage young men from coming to us for only a few months in order to get our certificate of graduation. Our desire is to have them with us as long as possible so that we may exert a more lasting influence. There is a growing religious interest also, and the Sunday evening preaching services and the Wednesday evening prayer meeting services are well attended. From fifty to sixty are regularly present at the ordinary Y. M. C. A. prayer meeting, and on Sundays and at special meetings the attendance is larger.

Owing to the increased number of students, the new ones being mostly non-Christians, the proportion of Christians is smaller than it has been for many years; being only about 1/5 of the whole. But this opens up greater opportunities for evangelistic work and we hope for good results. Four of our pupils have been baptized during the year. In every way we feel much encouraged and are thankful to our God for the good way in which he is leading us."

Mr. Ballagh:—"Concerning the several stations under my care, there are very few conversions, little or no advance in self-support, increased salaries and expenses connected with each out-station. The gracious wave of blessing felt in the cities has not yet reached the country districts. It is possibly the lack of interest on the part of the superintendent evangelist, in my own case at least ; but not feeling equal to the task, I see no help for it. A further palsying effect is the severe cut our mission has experienced with the opening year of the century. It has debarred us from taking any very aggressive steps in evangelistic efforts. With thankfulness I can report a very good state of feeling with workers in the various fields. All seems harmonious, with some increase of interest and attendance on the part of the public. We must deplore the lack of workers in several long worked, but practically abandoned fields. There are several such, where once church organizations existed, with now but a handful of believers living practically without the gospel. They are not oblivious of their loss, and plead for gospel privileges. I enclose you a copy of deficient statistics. Eight churches formerly under the care of the mission, are now self-supporting, and several have passed under other oversight. Owing to engagements in connection with the evangelistic movement in Tokyo and Yokohama I found it impossible to visit in person the south Shin-hu field in latter part of May. I was made very happy by Rev. R. E. McAlpine of the Southern Presbyterian Mission consenting to visit the field in my place. The results of his visit at Mat-umoto, at Suwa, at Ina, and at Iida were very satisfactory to the workers and to the people generally, as well as to the mission in the economy of his travelling expenses."

Mr. Booth:—" Ferris Seminary, Yokohama, is a Christian private school for Japanese girls, established in 1875, by the Board of Foreign Missions of the Reformed Church in America. It has three departments at present : The Preparatory of three years; the Grammar Course of four years; and the Bible Course of two years. The Higher Course was discontinued five years ago, owing to the financial inability of the mission to maintain it. The opening of the Higher Course, however, has been authorized on condition that an endowment of forty thousand yen can be secured. The present financial condition in Japan is far from reassuring for the success of such an undertaking within any reasonable time in the near future. The teachers are the Rev. and Mrs. Booth in charge : Miss Julia Moulton and Miss Harriet Wyckoff. The latter is taking Miss A. de F. Thompson's place while she is absent on furlough. There are also five Japanese teachers, a matron and three who teach special branches. There were sixty-five pupils in attendance last year, in all departments. There are at present eighty-three enrolled, distributed at follows :—Bible Course, 3 ; Grammar Course, 63 ; Preparatory Course, 17, Total, 83. Of this number thirty-eight are Christians ; seven have been baptized during the year. Nearly all the others are earnestly inquiring. The prospects for the school both as regards numbers, scholarship, and what is more important, development of Christian life and character were never better. Of my personal work aside from giving instruction in the Bible Course and the management of the school I am pastor of the Union Church, Yohohama. In regard to that work I have little to report. Souls have been strengthened and encouraged, and some I believe have found light and life through faith in our Saviour. My Bible class of foreign young men has grown : from sixteen to twenty attend. The organization from the members of the Bible class of a chapter of the Brotherhood of Andrew and Philip has been of great assistance and has proved a means of grace to the young men themselves. On the first of May a daily noon day service of prayer for twenty minutes was opene l at No. 60-e Main St., Yokohama. This is under the auspices of the Brotherhood. It is destined, I believe, to be a valuable means of grace. An appointment with God for busy men."

Mr. Scudder:—"The work and workers in Nagano and vicinity have passed through deep waters during the greater part of the past year. It is not that decided encouragements and items of interest have been lacking in the midst of the darkest hours of trial, but the impossibility of presenting in a report the events through which the church, the Japanese Christians and the missionaries together have been passing make us feel that any report which could be given would would be only misleading. Excepting, therefore the cheerful testimony to God's unfailing love and faithfulness, no further report is submitted."

Miss Winn:—"After a year's furlough in America, I was glad to return in Nov. 1900 to Aomori, my old station. As in former years, my work has been chiefly with the women and children. I have also had classes with the young men in English and Bible study. We have four flourishing Sunday-schools, the attendance at which falls off somewhat during the summer months : but during the winter months, often the rooms we rent are unable of accommodate the numbers of children and grown people who pour in. Thus far this year, there has been no great ingathering of souls. Only three have asked for baptism. But the numbers of inquirers are steadily growing. We have three young men in the church who are proving treasures as helpers in Sunday-school work, etc. They are all officials, but whenever off duty, are more than willing to lend me their services. They often give up their evenings to help me explain the life of Christ through magic-lantern pictures. We have two grandmothers who are pillars in our church. One has for years been bed-ridden and is now only able to move the muscles on of her hands and neck, but is rich in simple, childlike faith. I feel sure that some of our conversions could be traced directly to her prayers. The other old woman is not so infirm ; and no wintry snow storm is able to prevent her coming out to the meetings. She also is mighty in prayer and assists us in house-to-house calling.

We have an interesting opening for work at Ono Mura. An old farmer, the head of the village, sends a messenger into Aomori from time to time to tell us that on such a day the farmers will have a holiday, and requests us come and tell the gospel story. He gathers the villagers together at his own house. His good wife always provides a bountiful dinner for us.

Thus the doors are opening far faster than we are able to enter. Everywhere I find the people more than ready to hear the gospel.

Bibles have been sold, tracts distributed ; and we have one and all tried to be faithful."

---

4. SOUTH JAPAN MISSION OF THE REFORMED (Dutch) CHURCH IN AMERICA.

STATION	POPULATION	KEN	POPULATION
Nagasaki	106574	Nagasaki Ken	895753
Kagoshima·	52956	Kagoshima Ken	1.099445
Saga	32266	Saga Ken	618703

DR. STOUT :—" Personally my time has been occupied largely in the routine duties of principal and instructor in Steele College. This has not been fruitful of interesting experiences; unless mention be made of what occurred at the death of a student, a martyr through poverty to the ambition for an education. But that is a story that would not fit into a report.

Connected with our Nagasaki station are two outstations. At these, and in Nagasaki itself, the work has gone on steadily and quietly. The church has suffered considerable losses through removals, but has gained more in numbers for a like cause ; viz. the influx of population, through the commercial prosperity of the place, bringing with it members of churches from other localities, who more frequently than formerly, show a disposition to identify themselves with the local church. They do not, however, bring much financial aid to the church.

The only change in methods that seems worthy of consideration is that in Steele College, bringing it more in line with Middle Schools of the country, in respect both to the courses of study and the calendar. This has evidently been appreciated by patrons, and it works well. There are now over a hundred students in attendance; the numbers in the five classes being fairly well distributed. The tone of the school is more decidedly Christian than it has been too frequently in the past. As to prospects, plans are under consideration to secure official recognition and the privileges accruing therefrom for Steele College. But in this matter, as well as in other ways, the mission is seriously hampered by lack of appropriations to push forward the work according to openings presented. Even this plan for the school would involve expense."

MR. OLTMANS :—" From the Bible School, which was held from May 1st to 10th, several of our men were absent by reason of illness in their families. On the other hand we had the Presbyterian men from Sanyo join us, and Mr. Curtis himself as well. Mr. Peeke also was present. The entire number attending was sixteen ; fourteen preachers and two Bible women. The subject studied was Jesus Christ in the Old and New Testaments. Of course only outline studies could be pursued during such a limited time. The interest taken by the men was great and sustained throughout. The manner of dealing with the questions that came up clearly shewed that many of them have a firm grasp of many of the vital truths of the Bible. We were helped not a little by the attendance of an evangelist from the north, Mr. Inoue who last year graduated from the Meiji Gakuin and is on his way to work in Hawaii among the Japanese. My firm conviction is that more ought to be done in the pure Bible study with the men with whom we labor. Sound, practical exegesis of the word lies at the basis of all solid evangelistic work.

As to the field in general, there is first a general readiness to hear the word preached, when it is brought in reach. The quietness with which audiences of unbelievers listen to the straight gospel is quite remarkable. Secondly a general spirit of inquiry which though it does not express itself largely in positive desire to become converted, is still a sure sign of the working of God's Spirit in that direction. Thirdly, the felt need among our Japanese workers of more spirituality in their own lives, and more of dependence on the Holy Spirit for success in the work. If I mistake not, this want is felt by many of the foreign missionaries. May it be speedily supplied. Fourthly, the nature of the candidates for baptism. They certainly are more satisfactory than they were formerly. This is due not a little to the care exercised by our Japanese brethren in the preparation of these candidates. It augurs well for the future permanence of the work of the Church. We have had some rather stricking cases of conversion in this field, yet not more striking than we ought to expect, if we all faithfully preach the word and live a pure life.

During the year I have been carrying on Bible classes, of Chu Gakko and Shihan Gakko students. This I do wholly as a secondary work, and only at the intervals of my being at home from my evangelistic trips. I may add that we have recently started a store in Saga for the sale of Bibles, hymn-books, and Christian literature. Thus far we sell in the line of books only the publications of the Methodist Publishing House on commission. There is prospect of success along this line, and we trust it will be a decided help in the work."

MR. PEEKE:—" We represent the Church of Christ in Japan in the southern third of Kyushu. We have plenty of territory, plenty of people, and a paucity of Christian workers, foreign and Japanese. Ours is a purely evangelistic station; those in charge are the Rev. and Mrs. H. V. S. Peeke and Miss H. M. Lansing. Mrs. Peeke devotes herself to language study and the kinds of evangelism that can have a fixed center in her own home. A women's meeting, a gathering of young girls to learn fancy-work and hear the gospel, and a Sunday-school have been her lines of activity. The readiness of the people to be friendly, attend classes, etc., has been exceedingly satisfactory.

Miss Lansing has studied the language a good deal, and besides has been active in calling herself and having others do evangelistic calling, and in carrying on three Sunday-school classes for children. She has reached upwards of a hundred and fifty children weekly. Here too we must say that there has been no marked hindrance to the putting forth of effort. The people are very kind and friendly. We have been surprised to find that often times every child in a whole family has come regularly to the Sunday-school for weeks. The parents not simply consenting but desiring the children to come.

Mr. Peeke has had charge of the general evangelistic work. We have one church organization; that at Kagoshima. Evangelists are stationed outside at Kawanabe, Miyakonojō, and Hitoyoshi. One extra evangelist has lived in Kagoshima, traveling to important places outside. One of these evangelists has become involved in business affairs and has resigned, and another is seriously ill; so next year we have a prospect of workers only at Kagoshima, Miyakonojō and the Kawanabe district.

Miyakonojō has had a prosperous year. The evangelist is of the right stuff, thoroughly grounds his inquirers on God's word; and there have been two good-men added to his roll this last year. A student has come from the Meiji Gakuin Theol. Dept. to teach English in the Chu Gakkō, and will be a help to the work. This field is stronger than ever before, and we anticipate still more improvement. The new additions are both veterinary surgeons and men belonging to the locality. Hitoyoshi is a city in the mountains with a handful of lukewarm Christians who united with the Church a dozen years ago. It is true that during the last couple of years there has been an increase in faithfulness on the part of several women of the company, but in general the field lies torpid. As the evangelist is ill, possibly not to recover, and we are short handed all around, we may be obliged to withdraw this year. Kawanabe has had its own difficulties, prominent among which is the fact that the evangelist, becoming involved in business matters in his adjacent home, has not been able to do his best. Still, in the whole broad field there are eight or ten people who are quite near if not over the threshold of the kingdom. A new evangelist takes up the work there this month; and it is our hope that within the coming year, these people may all come out clearly on the Lord's side The field is distinctly promising. In regard to this country work it may be said that while it does not show up much even now, yet in territory that was Egyptian darkness six years ago, there are here and there Christians, and a good many people who know more or less accurately what Christianity stands for.

We have had a good year in Kagoshima City. Our Sunday audiences have numbered thirty and over right along, but we are facing a different prospect just now. During the last two months we have lost by removal ten of our most faithful workers and attendants; among them an elder, and Miss Lansing who goes home on furlough. But even with that the outlook is promising. There are many friends of our work, the church Sunday-school is prosperous, and we have a well located church building. We have had more baptisms during the last year than for some time, and we expect a number to be added during the coming year. Those who come in now have a stauncher faith than formerly, and most of them have a good knowledge of Scripture. The report of the church will be found in the report of the Chinzei Presbytery. I may say that since January our church Sunday-school has numbered about forty.

There is an excellent feeling among the three Churches at work here. This has been shown markedly in the Taikyo Dendo. The

61

workers have banded together to go out in a company of four to six, walking to save expense, and plan to visit and hold meetings in about sixty of the principal places in the *Ken*. We have visited about twenty of these places already, have had good meetings and distributed much literature. We have a kind reception everywhere. It is worthy of remark that many people are become unsatisfied with being religionless and are asking intelligently and interestedly about our teaching We have practically no difficulty in obtaining places for these Taikyo Dendo meetings; and the best of attention is accorded to us everywhere. In short, we have nothing to hinder us from going right ahead to proclaim the gospel as far as we have strength and money to defray expenses."

5. Mission of the Presbyterian Church in the U.S. (Southern).

STATION.	POPULATION.	FU OR KEN.	POPULATION.
Nagoya	233771	Aichi Ken ⎫	1628777
Okazaki	16884	,, ,, ⎬	
Kobe	214119	Hyogo ,,	1708646
Tokushima	60668	Tokushima Ken	687254
Takamatsu	34416	Kagawa ,,	687768
Kochi	35538 ⎫	Kochi ,,	620061
Susaki	5000 ⎭		

Mr. McAlpine:—"Old lines of work were continued during the past year and some new methods have also been tried. Among the new plans one was playing base-ball and tennis with Middle School boys and local officials. Some fun but no other results visible. A much more important new work was Bible-selling. Getting us a small supply of Scriptures I sold to visitors at my house, especially those that professed to have come to learn about Christianity; the people living in the neighborhood, at chappel meetings, and meetings during country tours; and quite a number of gospels to passengers on trains. At present I have a stock of Scriptures on hand at my house and deposited with various workers through the country. This has been decidedly an interesting work. In this connection I have been trying to get the Christians interested in the O. T. and to own a complete Bible instead of a New Testament. To help on this I have often preached from the O.T., and had Sabbath afternoon classes in the Pentateuch at my house. Whenever at home I have taught a Bible class at the Girls school, also irregular classes of students and soldiers, especially after Miss Wimbish had to give up her afternoon class on account of ill health. Many of those young men came to me until they found how often I was absent. In Feb. a gentleman came to my door and asked to study the Bible.

He wanted to bring his wife. They have come regularly ever since studying Matthew in Japanese and have attended our services a few times. We hope they will prove real seekers after God. An energetic young Christian has held a children's meeting at our house every Sabbath throughout the year. The state of the Aioicho Chapel work is still "great expectation." The Tachibana Cho Chapel is as usual a good place to sow the seed, but no place to reap. We want to give more attention to it and make it a more attractive place the coming year.

In the country the work began last year at Kurokawa, the secluded mountain hamlet where I was the third foreigner ever to go, has gone on and resulted this spring in the baptism of one man, a well-to-do farmer who seemed to seriously examine the truth and accepted it as he learned it. With two strong Christians there now we hope for further progress. After long efforts we have been able to take up work at Tajimi a pottery manufacturing town; one that was right on our way to our old work. A former official of the town bought a complete Bible last November, and read it through three times by February adding his own notes. Recently he said he was ready definitely to declare himself a Christian and I hope soon to examine him more particularly as to his faith. The older work at Nakatsu Gawa is slowly recovering from a church quarrel. At Oii Mura there are three solid noble Christians with their families and several hopeful inquirers, and a good harmonious spirit among them all. At Imamura three or four of our best Christians have been drafted into the army or have removed. So that good old Kato the preacher is somewhat discouraged. The Seto church has just erected a new house of worship; is largely self-supporting and in quite good condition. The Kitagori work, decidedly languished because of no regular visits being made there. But recently arrangements have been made to systematically visit that field. During the year I have baptized four adults and one infant.

The Nagoya church is in a fairly good condition. It has been self-supporting for years. The pastor Mr. Sakakura is a man of most excellent spirit; and the relation is most happy between him and us foreign workers. Among the members the Devil got a chance to make trouble last winter; but I hope he has been driven out of their hearts again as peace seems to be reigning once more. If they were only more alive to their privileges and duties one would be happier over them."

MR. CUMMING :—" I have three groups of country fields known as the Takigahama, Gifu, and Kaneyama fields. During an industrial exhibition held in Gifu during April and May of this year, for thirty days we had special services in one preaching place twice every day, in the afternoon and at night. Many people from the country districts heard the gospel for the first time. Nearly 2000 copies of a tract specially prepared for the occasion were distributed at that time. Two visiting brethren from Tokyo made a trip through these different fields, and had good and attentive audiences."

MISS HOUSTON :—" Since the last Council meeting a nice lot has been purchased for the school; the buildings have been moved and much improvement made in every way. There have been fifty-one pupils during the year. Four graduated at the last commencement, and there were thirty-seven in school at the last of April. There are twelve church members in the school, and nine others have become Christians during the year, but have not yet been received into the Church. Of twenty-eight graduates, eight are teachers, three are in evangelistic work, and thirteen have been married."

MR. MYERS:—"In the last twelve mouths we have had our forces increased by Miss Annie Patton, who came out from America last December, and by two Japanese Bible women. We now have one male, and three female missionaries, two evangelists, and three Bible women. At the time of our last report, we had bought property on a good street in the central part of the city, and we hoped to get our building in some four or five years. In the meantime, we made good use of the three buildings on the lot. The rents from the two shops in front swelled our income, and the residence in the rear was occupied by one of the evangelists and used for our services. This arrangement proved to be eminently unsatisfactory, as the rear building could be reached only by a dark narrow passage. So the building was almost useless for active evangelistic work. This spring we decided that we must go ahead and get our building at once. We made known our wants to our country Christians, our missionary friends, and a few friends at home. The response was prompt and liberal; and now a stranger visiting the city may see on Tori Machi a stone foundation on which a large and handsome church is to be erected perhaps by the time the Council meets. This work has not been all plain-sailing; as some thought the money couldn't be raised, and it was foolish to try. Some did not like to be asked for large contributions again so soon after buying the lot; some thought the church should be built in Japanese style; etc. Our troubles may not be over yet, but we hope they are.

' In the city we still have meetings on two evenings in the week in our Shinmachi chapel. This is well located for seed sowing, and we generally have large audiences. Besides there are seven meetings weekly in different parts of the city for women and children. We are just starting a plan of renting a building in the unevangelized section of the city, and holding nightly services for a week. The attendance at our first attempt was most encouraging.

In the country our work is embarrassed by the lack of workers. As heretofore we have weekly meetings at Komatsujima, seven miles south of Tokushima; and there are quite a number of hopeful inquirers. Recently a Christian from the Sendai church was discovered here. He had been teaching in the province for years, but hid the fact that he had been baptized. He recently confessed his sin and repented. We have services as often as possible in several villages near Komatsujima. On the railroad we have weekly meetings at Ishi, eight miles west of the city. One of our Christians has greatly assisted in the meetings here and in the neighboring villages.

Our most distant work is in a group of towns from 40 to 60 miles west of the city, which I have tried with varying success to visit once a month. Miss F. D. Patton has gone out to this field often, and spent

64

weeks at a time there. With a good worker such as we are praying the Lord to send, this field promises to be one of the most fruitful in the whole province. In the past twelve months, we have had seven adults, and two children added to the church by baptism; and one baptized in infancy, received into full communion. It is perhaps worthy of note that two of these are members of my English class."

Miss Patton:—"My work is entirely among women and children. For the former I have two meetings a week; for the latter, from four to seven. Besides these I have a monthly meeting for women, and also a class in the Sunday-school. A considerable part of my time is given to visiting and teaching."

Mr. Fulton:—"The work of the Okazaki station for the past year has been remarkable for the *lack* of any specially striking results rather than for the presence of such results. We have never yet been able to shake the dead conservatism of the place. The Hongwanji sect of Buddhism has the field, and it has managed so far to hold it. Still there are some signs of a growing desire to hear of Christianity. With all the Buddhist conservatism of the place we have never had any open, violent opposition.

For the past nine months we have been without the help of a Japanese worker and this has thrown the burden of the work on the resident missionary. On account of this lack of workers the country districts have for the most part been "resting." We have tried to keep up the work in some of them, and we hope to have a worker before long.

Here in Okazaki we carry on two preaching places, a woman's meeting, a young men's association, and various classes for Bible study. The women have made commendable progress in the raising of money for the building of a church. The Christians are fairly faithful in their attendance on the church services, but are lacking in the spirit of working for the unconverted. Besides Okazaki there are two other places which have small bands of Christians and which we try to make centers of work. In one of these an evangelist is located and some little progress has been made. The other is without a worker and the work is stationary.

On the whole, there is not much to encourage the hope for immediate results, but we believe that the Lord will yet make his name known here."

Mr. Price:—"The last year has been marked by progress in all the different lines of church work. I say church work because having no school work except private classes, and unfortunately having no country work, all the work of the mission is closely connected with the church. Our church, which became entirely self-supporting from the 1st of July 1900, has been able to meet its financial obligations which have been heavy, closing the year with perhaps only eight or ten *yen* indebtedness. The church membership has largely increased by baptisms and by letter; so that at present there are about 180 adults enrolled in the church and preaching place. Besides there are a large number who have not yet transferred their membership. The church attendance has increased, but unfortunately not in proportion to the increase in membership. The work has been extended by establishing a preaching-place for the church in Hyogo in the lower part of the city. There are twenty members enrolled there with promise of increase in the near future. An evangelist is in charge of this work. It is proposed to open a chapel in the eastern part of the city and we hope that eventually these two centers of work will become churches.

A portion of the church is filled with the spirit of work; and if all were of the same mind we could expect even greater things than we have seen in the past three years. The four noticeable things in our work during the past year have been: (1) Large increase in contributions; (2) large increase in membership; (3) the spirit of earnest hard work for non-Christians; (4) the willingness of non-Christians to hear about Christianity.

The missionaries have worked along the same lines as before: i.e. night classes in English and Bible for the young men, meetings during the week for children, woman's meetings, preaching, and house-to-house visiting. House-to-house visiting I consider the work promising best results. For the first time in Kobe our mission has done systematic house-to-house work, block by block. The evangelist in Hyogo has visited in this way with Mr. Price, distributing tracts and speaking a word to the people. A plan was proposed to the churches in Kobe to visit every house in Kobe this year; but I do not think it will be done. The Taikyo Dendo movement has more or less influenced all classes of work, except school class work. It has drawn the churches of all denominations nearer together than ever before. So that the spirit of union is very delightful to see. Union preaching services have been frequent, and most of the churches seem to feel free to call upon each other for help which is gladly given. House-to-house visiting, distribution of leaflets, lectures, both as union meetings and as conducted by the different churches, have been the usual forms of work up to the present. Heretofore these lectures were held for only one or two nights; and the plan was to have different speakers each time. But the idea is growing that more good will be done if they are held for several days with one or two preaching continuously. I heartily approve of this idea as it gives a minister an opportunity to develop a line of thought. The most striking change has been however in the method of advertising the meetings, and the methods of seeking for visible results. As this change started from Tokyo and has met with most remarkable success there, the Tokyo reports will bring out the plan in full. Kobe is but the echo of what is being done in Tokyo. It is indeed a remarkable thing in Kobe to have the refined and educated and popular pastors of the churches of all denominations, including the Episcopalians of the S. P. G. Mission, marching with a hundred Christians through the city carrying lanterns, singing christian hymns and advertising the meetings to be held in all the Churches. This is what is being done at present in Kobe, to be followed by meetings in all the churches and chapels next week. During a meeting in our church a band of Sunday-school boys led by three or four young men, one of whom had an accordion, went through the streets singing Christian hymns which sounded very well indeed. As a result partly of this method of advertising and of the earnest work being done, the

66

meetings in all the churches are large and I think the poor are having the gospel preached to them as never before. I believe that we are on the eve of a general revival with the expectation of rich results. Now is the time for preaching of the simplest and most direct kind, when as never before preaching of another kind seems so utterly out of place and even wrong.

The need of pastoral work of the most devoted and earnest kind, is called for now as never before; and if the Church fails in that point the harvest will be proportionally small. Already there are thousands of ex-church members to be found all over the land. Fruitless limbs are in all our churches which might be made fruit bearing branches again with proper leading and the blessing of the Holy Spirit. One of the most pleasant features of the series of meetings, recently held in our church was the home class for women in the houses of our missionaries. The preachers came and spoke to the ladies and it was a real pleasure to have a number of refined ladies in the neighborhood attend these classes. They were held at 9.30 A.M. The largest number of non-Christians attending any one of these meetings not including the servants in the missionaries family was eleven. Amid all the work, zeal, and progress we are sad to report a great lack of Sabbath observance; and we feel that the blessings will be less than they would if we all remembered the Sabbath day to keep it holy."

Mr. WALTER McS. BUCHANAN :—" For awhile, owing to the scarcity of workers, we had only two Sunday-schools; but now have four. We have used the chain cards and the *saiwai* cards of the Tokima Sha much to the pleasure and interest of the scholars. In our main Sunday-school, that of the chapel in Takamatsu, there is one very encouraging feature : viz. the large number of adults. The Christians both men and women attend the Bible classes very well, setting indeed a very good example to those at home, where young people as they grow up graduate from the Sunday-school. The missionaries and evangelists of course take part in the Sunday-school ; and I am glad to report that now among the Christians there are others who take classes. We are not yet doing what we wish to do in the Sunday-school work ; for we realize its importance more and more, especially as we consider the wonderful results of the special efforts that have been made in Tokyo, Yokohama and other places, where multitudes have come out in open profession of faith in the Lord Jesus Christ. For in this we see the fruits by the blessing of the Holy Spirit of much seed sowing in years past in which the Sunday-school doubtless has had a large share. I have more and more confidence in the success, more joy in the work, and recognize more and more the importance of Sunday-school work. This training of the young in the plastic period of life, this training of the little children whom the Lord himself did not despise but took up in his arms and blessed.

Whether it be attendance on the services of the sanctuary or manifest zeal and faith, we are glad to report improvement in the spiritual life of the Christians. Family worship is maintained in nearly every home where the head is a Christian. The Sabbath also is generally kept holy. The faith and zeal of the private Christians were made manifest in the prayers, exhortations, and invitations to relatives and friends. Indeed a number of the conversions this year were due to the influence of private Christians. We rejoice not only that they recognize the responsibility resting upon them, but that they enjoy the privilege of leading others to our adorable Lord. The additions for the term under report are 53 adults, 8 being by letter; and 17 children baptized. The contributions too have been increased; and the Christians in their zeal propose building a church for which liberal contributions have been made. In regard to general evangelistic work, I might say that up to last November we were greatly hampered for lack of workers. But at the end of November the Rev. W. C. Buchanan returned from a furlough; and besides we have increased the members of Japanese evangelists. So we feel greatly strengthened and encouraged and hope to covers the whole field of Sanuki more thoroughly still. Our usual method in out-stations and country towns is to have street preaching; distributing tracts inviting to night meeting in the afternoon, and then a meeting at night in the chapel if there be one, or in our hotel. Last spring we combined our forces for about a week on Takematsu, the Congregational evangelist of a neighboring town visiting with us. Every morning we had sun-rise prayer meetings on behalf of the work of the day. The Christians largely attended and these prayer meetings brought great blessing to all apparently. Returning home for breakfast the missionaries and evangelists again met at 8 or 8:30 o'clock at the chapel, whence parting into two companies we went out for street preaching, distributing tracts etc. We had the street preaching in the morning so as to give the speakers a little rest before the night service, lest their throats should give out. During this period of special effort in the city, when in five days over a hundred sermons and sermonettes were preached, our usual experience in country towns was repeated: viz. good audiences and a respectful hearing.

The Christians too took an active part in extending invitations, distributing tracts, etc. Besides two brethren opened their shops for night meetings. We also managed to rent two other places for night meetings. Extensive work in this province is comparatively new; so this work is largely seed sowing. But we believe the word of the Lord concerning his word that "It shall not return unto me void but it shall accomplish that which I please; and shall prosper in the thing whereto I sent it." Hence we may hope for a more abundant harvest some day."

Mr. W. C. BUCHANAN:—"Mention should be made of the classes that have been held by the missionaries in their homes. English classes have been conducted with a fairly good attendance of young men, also classes for officials and school teachers. Every one who joined these classes was distinctly informed that we would expect him to appear at one of the Sunday services, and for the most part the members of the classes kept their promise pretty well. The result was all that could be expected. They got used to attending Christian services and at the same time much prejudice was in this way overcome, and some few have become Christians. Our missionary wives too have conducted English and Bible classes at home as well as Bible classes in the Sunday-schools. In all instances the ladies have confined themselves to work among women and girls; with the result, if we mistake not, that the impression is growing that Christianity does not necessarily make women forward and mannish."

MR. McILVAINE:—"There has been little or no change in methods or progress since last year; and the same report might answer for this. My work has been about the same as last year.

A series of trips to country places where people have not heard the gospel, and visiting little groups of Christians here and there. There have not been many visible results. I have baptized during the year only one adult and four children. There are several interesting inquirers whom we hope to receive into the Church ere long. Progress has been impeded in some quarters by doubtful practices of professed Christians, and in others by gross immorality on the part of these who should be lights. While coldness and indifference on the part of a great majority do not render the situation any more hopeful. There is a sign of and a reason for hope of better things in the faithful few upon whom God has set his mark, and who sigh and cry for the abominations that are committed. We thank God and take courage that there are such.

Miss Atkinson taught two children's meetings, visited among the women, and did something in Bible selling and tract distribution. Miss Dowd paid two visits to this field and did a great deal to encourage the women both in Kochi and in the country places.

The church here reports six baptisms during year and nineteen received by letter. The two companies of Christians at Gomen and Aki that have been self-supporting up to this time are now without preachers. Mr. Tada preaches to the former an Sabbath afternoons. The meetings at Aki are kept up by the people themselves; the missionary and his helper going as often as other engagements permit. The great need here is a revival of pure and undefiled religion."

MR. MOORE:—"Nothing new, only the old ways of work. During the most of the year, from sickness and various meetings, I was confined a good deal to Susaki; and the work in the outside stations has been more neglected than usual. The interest in Susaki, is still quite encouraging, though more quiet than formerly, owing to the fact of the newness having worn off somewhat. Until the first of June there have been two licensed evangelists, but one having removed to another of our stations. I got an elder in the Kochi church to help in the outside work as well as the work in Susaki as occasion required. There are encouraging signs on almost every side, but only one of our outstations as shown any marked signs of interest. The fact is, except two villages, worked formerly from Kochi, my present field is new; and outside of these and Susaki there are not a half a dozen Christians all told. In short Susaki is not yet ready to report. A good deal of preaching to quiet attentive audiences has been done; but we still wait for God's special blessing upon comparatively recent seed-sowing. We are hoping and praying for similar showers such as have fallen in other places.

6. Mission of the Reformed (German) Church in the U. S.

STATION	POPULATION	KEN	POPULATION
Sendai	75256	Miyagi Ken	843010

Mr. Noss:—" We have had an encouraging year, the only drawback being the inadequacy of the missionary force. The only missionaries able to do any touring have been Dr. Schneder and the writer. The mission has had two accessions, Brothers Lampe and Faust; but they have been kept at home studying the language. Hitherto Dr. DeForest of the American Board has helped us generously in our evangelistic work. A number of professors of the Tohoku Gakuin are taking a deep interest in the work and do all the touring that their strength allows. The most active are Prof. Kajiwara, Dr. Sasao, Mr. Saito, Mr. Igarashi and Mr. Tanaka. Not including student-evangelists, there are on the pay-roll of the mission, twenty-four evangelists. There are three who do the work of an evangelist at their own charges, and two who get their salary entirely from the congregations they serve (Sendai and Hakodate). The number has scarcely varied for several years; we rarely lose are evangelist. Next year we shall have seven graduates from our own Theological Seminary, of whom at least five expect to enter our own evangelistic service. The salaries are, as a rule, 20 yen for unmarried men and 24 yen for married men, with an allowance for rent, children, or anything but travel. These salaries are larger than any where in the south, on account of the severity of the climate.

There have been a great many changes in location. As the younger evangelists gain experience, we pursue the policy of increasing the number of stations assigned them, believing that this is the only way to further the cause of self-support in the country. In this way also we have managed to supply all the points in the Tohoku field that have ever been worked by our mission.

Ashita and Yeira, our most distant and difficult points, have been assigned to our two oldest and most efficient evangelists. We have also opened a new station at Omiya, just north of Tokyo, and hope soon to place an evangelist and Shinyo in Yamagata Ken, the largest place in the north non yet supplied with a Christian worker. For the strengthening of our evangelists, we have started an annual conference in the fall, October or November. The mission pays the expenses, amounting in all, to yen 120. The effect is great encouragement all around. Two or three of our evangelists are about to leave our work were fully restored and filled with new zeal. For our twelve English reading evangelists, we have started an English circulating library. The books are selected by a committee of the professors of the Tohoku Gakuin, and twelve carefully chosen English periodicals, passed along the line, The members can pay little more than the postage. The evangelists themselves have started a little paper, designed to draw our people closer together.

Taikyo Dendo is the topic of the hour. We had very successful meetings in Sendai. The result has been the awakening of the city, and a quickening of the churches. In July, with the Rev. Yoichi Honda and Dr. Sasao, I hope to make a tour of Yamagata Ken. The work there has, in the absence of Mr. Miller, been suffering somewhat from neglect. Mr. Miller expects to return in the fall.

My work is, first in the Tokoku Gakuin, where I lecture in English and in Japanese; mostly on theological and Biblical subjects. I am Secretary of the mission. I do some touring, and preach on the average once a week. I have charge of the second church in Sendai, which possesses a fine chapel, and seems to have a bright future before it; its location being destined to become more and more, the residence portion of the city. The old Sendai Church is, with the aid of Dr. and Mrs. Schneder, completing an edifice which is one of the finest buildings of its kind in the country. We have two other principal preaching places in the city, aided by Prof. Gerhard, and Mr. Lampe."

Dr. SCHNEDER:—"I write first about our school for young men, the Tohoku Gakuin. The number of students has been about ninety until recently; the smallest number we have had for years. But in other respects, the school has been satisfactory. We have a good corps of teachers; all except two being Christians. The work of the school was carried on well; the religious condition has been good. Bible classes, prayer meetings, and other religious meetings for students were well attended. The number of baptisms was twelve. There is an active Y. M. C. A. in the school. Many of the students also engage in Sunday-school work. The inflow of students at the opening of the new school year in April was encouraging. We now have 142 students. The whole number of Christians is forty; the number of theological students eleven. The school has applied to the Department of Education for such recognition as will give it postponement of military conscription; and we have good hopes of getting it. This would give the school a forward impetus. We have a general course covering five years, corresponding to the ordinary five years course of a Middle School; a literary department covering two years; a theological Department, comprising two courses—an English and a Japanese course. The English course is for the graduates of the English Department. We are becoming more and more convinced of the great work a mission school has to do. My work has been largely that of attending to a multitude of small affairs. So for as I have been able to engage in preaching, I have found eager and ready audiences. The year's work has been on the whole more pleasant than usual; largely on account of the more respectful attitude of the people. In the city, my wife and I have come in contact with officials and others of high standing. These invariably show a favorable spirit toward Christianity."

Mr. FAUST:—"I came to Japan September 3rd, 1900. I teach church history in the English course of the Tohoku Gakuin, devote most of my time to the study of the Japanese language and superintend our Sunday-school at Nagamachi. During the last half year, the attendance has increased about 25%. We have now over 100 scholars enrolled. I am teaching two English Bible classes. These classes are composed of students from the Koto Gakko and our own school. The

71

one class numbers 20, the other 12. I have made two evangelistic trips, on which occasions I spoke through an interpreter. In Sendai I have preached a number of times. The Lord is prospering his work in our hands, and we have all reason to be thankful to him."

Mr. Lampe:—" Mrs. Lampe and I have been in Japan only a year and a half, and are therefore unable to undertake much important direct missionary work. My time for the first year was given almost exclusively to the study of the language. I made some progress, I am happy to say, but can not yet preach in Japanese. I suppose ours is not the only mission of which is true that the workers are too few. On account of other work, Dr. Schneder resigned the treasurership of our mission last January, and although I had been in Japan a little less than a year, I was elected in his stead. This business work and the oversight of a house we are now building make me sometimes ask myself, if this is the missionary work I came to Japan to do. I suppose it is part of it. At any rate, it takes some of my time, and hence forms a part of this report.

By the direction of our mission and Board, I am to give my main strength and time to the study of the language, and at the same time to teach in the Tohoku Gakuin not more than ten hours per week. I am teaching the English Bible and English Rhetoric in the Academic Department, and New Testament Greek in the Theological Department of the Tohoku Gakuin. I also have charge of the Aiamachi preaching-place in Sendai. I am reported to the authorities as evangelist there; but Japanese do most of the preaching. When I preach, a friend interprets for me. We have an average attendance of 60 children in the Sunday-school; and on Sunday night at the preaching service an average attendance of 16 adults. At the Aiamachi preaching-place, on March 30th, I had the great joy of baptizing seven policemen, whom I taught for several hours a week for several months. They are an earnest, faithful band of young men, and are not ashamed to let it be known that they are Christians. Not only are the prospects in the north very bright, but we are actually in the very midst of a harvest. There is great joy in the work for the Master in this part of his vineyard. Our mission has called for the appointment of ten more missionaries, to be sent within the next five years."

Mr. Snyder:—"During the year I have been enabled to sell over 70,000 of the little gospels and about 1000 Bibles and Testaments. I have traveled 20700 miles in 41 different provinces. With me it has been constant seed-sowing. I see little of the fruit; yet some is traceable to this work, and in other places it bears fruit if we cannot see it. Much of my work has been on the R R., though I have sold in many different ways. A trip with the Rev. Mr. Allchin last fall was very interesting. During the day we sold the gospels and also tracts in the streets; then in the evening at the magic lantern lecture we also sold. I believe much good was done by combining the selling of the gospels with the magic lantern meetings. Now I am going along with the Taikyo Dendo workers. We do all we can during the day working in the streets and going from house to house. Thus many are sold. We also sell in the evening at the meetings. Yesterday in Hirose we had a force of twelve, missionaries evangelists and Christians, selling gospels in the street. Thus the written and spoken word go out together. In Kyoto and Osaka many hundreds were sold from a little table placed in the street, selling to those who passed by.

All classes seem open and ready to receive the printed word, and they seem no less ready to hear. We certainly have much for which to give thanks."

Miss Weidner:—" Formerly our school year began in September and ended in June. Some years ago it was decided to conform with the public school year. The last class under the old system graduated in June of last year when eleven girls received their diplomas. The school year for all classes now runs from April to March. The school includes three departments, the Preparatory Department with a three years course corresponding to the Koto Sho-Gakko; the Academic Department corresponding to the Koto Jo-Gakko and a Post-Graduate Department of one year.

When the last report of the school was made Miss Lena Zurfluh was in charge of the school alone. In June of last year she was joined by Miss Sadie Lea Weidner and in September by Miss Lucy Margaret Powell. In December Miss Zurfluh returned to America on furlough and Miss Weidner was elected to take her place in her absence. Miss Kathryn Pifer is expected in the fall.

During the past school year, April 1900 to March 1901, there were sixty-five girls enrolled, eleven in the Preparatory Department; forty-three in the Regular Department; and eleven in the Post-Graduate. In March eight girls graduated; five of whom are now engaged in Bible work; one is a tutor in our school; one is a student in the recently established Joshi Dai-Gakko and one is at home. In April when the new term opened thirty new girls were admitted. The present enrollment is fourteen in the Preparatory Department; fifty-three in the Regular Department; and seventeen in the Post Graduate Department; a total of eighty-four.

The past year has been a very prosperous one. The attendance has been very large, the number admitted this spring being the largest in the history of the school. The respect of the people of Sendai has been won year by year until now the value of the school is receiving very general recognition. Of the thirty new girls twenty-two are from Sendai. Every year sees more and more self-supporting girls.

The interest of the students in Bible study, Sunday-school and Church work is one of the most hopeful signs. During the year eleven girls were baptized. Of the sixty-five enrolled last year forty-three are baptized Christians. Of our thirty-nine graduates, thirty-eight are baptized Christians. Of the thirty new students none are Christians, a large field for work."

73

7. Mission of the Cumberland Presbyterian Church.

STATION	FU OR KEN	POPULATION
Osaka	Osaka Fu	1591221
Wakayama		
Tanabe	} Wakayama Ken	671432
Shingu		
Tsu	Mie Ken	995152

Dr. A. D. Hail:—"My work during the past year has been prosecuted with some drawbacks, not however arising from adverse circumstances in the field itself. The fact is that so far as the field itself is concerned, there is much that is encouraging. People seem to be very willing to hear the word, and to make intelligent and urgent inquiries concerning Christianity. Teachers in government schools, and well-to-do men of affairs seem to feel the need of a higher standard of morals for their country, and of a power to enable them to attain to such standards. These perhaps approach the consideration of the Christian Faith more from the standpoint of its value to produce a higher moral life than from almost any other point of view. Our preaching audiences have been more nearly composed of solid men, with a conviction of moral defectiveness and moral needs, than at any other time in the history of the work. Another feature of the work in my district has been the proportionately large attendance of men at the preaching services. At one point, out of 20 who designated their desire to receive instruction as catechumens there was but one woman. At new points opened in the interior the audiences have been almost invariably composed of men. Young men are also much more approachable than formerly.

There is a disposition on the part of evangelists, pastors and the lay members, to plan and pray for a working spirit and a deeper spiritual life. There seems to be a growing desire also for self-support. As an example of this, our Osaka East Church was taken under the care of the Synod's Board of Home Missions, beginning with December 1900, on condition that the church would furnish one-half the pastor's support the first year; three-fourths the second year: and with the beginning of the third year become entirely self-sustaining. After six months however, the church assumed the entire support of the pastor, and asked for his installation.

In the churches and older chapels, the Sunday-schools show an encouraging improvement; and there is a growing appreciation of this arm of the work, as an evangelizing and preservative factor in the church's life and work. Another encouraging aspect of the work is the increasing number of Christians in the older churches of the second generation. These have had Christian training, such as their fathers and mothers could not have, both in the family and afterwards in Christian schools. These are becoming more and more a source of comfort and help to the whole Church life and work. This state of

74

things makes a constantly growing amount of work to be done, both by missionaries and the Japanese Church. The readiness to work and assume responsibility upon the part of the Church, the widening of the opportunities for work, and the great increase of the numbers desirous of hearing the gospel, make it necessary to increase the number of evangelists pastors Bible women and other workers, especially if we aim at the speedy evangelization of Japan. On the other hand, the increasing expense of living and of travelling, puts the financial problem before us more prominently than before. At least, this is the paramount problem in my own field. For instance, in the Province of Ise, in the large towns of Matsuzaka, Yamada, and Toba, I have one evangelist who is trying to do the work of three men. Each place is too important to abandon, and the work is growing in interest. In Yamada, the seat of the great Ise Shrines, we have a little band of faithful Christians, who are working most earnestly. Two of these are engaged in prison work, and are furnished every encouragement and facility for their work by the officers of a prison so clean and well kept as to be worthy of all praise. The importance of maintaining men in such places in unquestionable, but the question is, "How can it be done on present allowances? This is one of the most serious questions confronting us in our work in this field.

In the City of Osaka, we have a field whose rapid growth in every direction presents another problem. New railroads opening out in all directions make it possible to follow them up in entering new points, easily accessible from the city as a centre. There seems to be an increasing need of central places of work, such as the Warren Kan, recently opened in the city by the C. M. S Mission. How to reach the tens of thousands of young men coming into the city, who are comparatively homeless, is another branch of the problem.

In view of the opportunities of the field, the openings for work, and the lack of corresponding increase of appropriations, there is a more than usual feeling that the annual chronic crisis in missions is still on hand. There is not simply the need of more missionaries, but also of a larger increase of allowances, that those on the field may do more extensive and more effective work. Of the two needs, the former, while indispensible, if lawful to use comparative terms, nevertheless leaves room for the statement, that the latter is much more so."

MR. JOHN E. HAIL:—" Having arrived in Osaka during the fall of 1900 my chief work has been the studying of the Japanese language. Outside of my study hours however I have been able to do some work. Three nights in the week I have taught English classes, giving two hours each evening to this work and half an hour to Bible work. As a result of this work five very promising young men have united with the East Church. Besides this I have called at something over 200 homes in the neighborhood of the East Church, inviting the people to attend our services. In no case have I been rudely received; and in only one instance was no promise given to attend the church services. After about six months of study I attempted my first Japanese sermon. It interested the audience greatly.

Under Dr. A. D. Hail's directions I have opened two preaching-places. The first is at Hirano, a suburb of Osaka. Other Churches had begun work in this place some years ago, but owing to a lack of success and bitter opposition had entirely abandoned the field. The town has the reputation of being a very wicked place. From the very beginning of the services until now, nearly three months, the preaching-place has not been able to hold the crowds which have gathered every Sunday. Probably the new type of Japanese to be heard is part of the attraction. The first visible fruits in this town have been a carpenter and a confectioner. The carpenter was first interested by a sermon on "The Good Father"—God's sacrifices for his wandering children appealing to the man's father-heart. The carpenter's increasing interest has been shown by the continual increase in his clothing from one service to the next. He is now clothed and in his right mind. This man and a confectioner being convinced of the truth of Christianity wished to know how much money they would be charged for entering the Christian Church. Their minds were fully made up to enter the Christian fold if they could possibly raise enough money to do so. They are now studying with a view to baptism. In this place I also conduct a Sunday afternoon Bible-class for some of the upper-class people whom we have not yet been able to persuade to attend the night services.

Nagano is a village of about 1500 people. It is at the end of the Koya railroad, twenty miles from Osaka. A member of our East Church returned to this place, his old home, to live. He asked me to come here, teach English as a bait, and preach, saying that if I would do so, I should be furnished with a house and an audience free of charge. I accepted the invitation and arranged for regular Saturday services. The people here rented a Buddhist temple, covered up the idols; and now Christian worship is carried on in this converted temple. These services are the first that have ever been held in this village. Commencing with about 27 in the English class and 60 at the preaching services, the English class has grown to over 40, and the attendance at the services has grown to over 80. After two and a half months' work we have five Christians and three baptized children, where before there was only one Christian. Besides these there are quite a number of inquirers studying Christianity. The people here are independent, self-respecting, and well-to-do. They have bought a number of Bibles and several commentaries. The outlook is very promising."

Mr. Van Horne:—"Returning to Japan only last December our report will be brief because of the time limit. Our work in Ajikawa Machi in Osaka could not receive the personal attention of the missionaries that we gave it, hence it was not as flourishing as we would like to have found it. This is no criticism on the evangelist Mr. Okamoto and his wife. They did faithful work. On our return in prayer and consultation with the evangelist and his wife, who is Mrs. Van Horne's helper, we began gathering up the loose ends and strengthening the weak points of this work. It was soon in good running order and so this work is now in better shape than for some-time. The Sunday-school also the preaching and prayer meeting services are well attended. In May we made a special effort to enter homes that hitherto were inaccessible. We gave a stereopticon entertainment to the children who interested their parents by their accounts of the scenes. Then while that interest still existed we followed up the impressions by giving one for the parents. On this occasion we prepared formal invitations, and Mrs. Van Horne and her Bible women went to the houses and delivered them in person. This brought out many, whom we had hitherto utterly failed to reach by any means. Our work began at once to show signs of awakening, and we soon had several interesting inquirers some of whom have asked for baptism. In June during the Taikyo Dendo campaign in Osaka we held a series of services for several weeks resulting in forty persons giving their names as inquirers. Most of them attended the services during these meetings. At two social meetings in the chapel many of them were present, and their conversation hinged absolutely on the gospel and the way of life. There were inquiry meetings in the true sense of the expression. These are all adults and with few exceptions have been visited at their homes. The work in Itami, a large village, sustains a good Sunday-school, and there are a number of inquirers. The work at this place is more hopeful as we have a Bible-woman living there. We have regular work in three villages in the Province of Izumi. Besides we visit five or six other villages as opportunity is afforded. We have a number of Christians and inquirers in this section. I baptized one very interesting convert at Tagawa in this province last May. In Kii we have regular work in four villages, and there are a number of others we visit occasionally. During our absence in America there was no resident evangelist here, and the work had not the benefit of Sunday services as formerly. However the work is moving on about as usual, and we have a number of interesting inquirers in this field. During this period we have distributed several thousand tracts and gospels. Especially do we find the Toki no Koe very interesting to our Christians and helpful in our work among inquirers.

The outlook in our different fields is more encouraging than ever before."

Miss Morgan:—"The statistics of the Wilmina Girls School are as follows: Pupils enrolled during the year, 60; Christian pupils, 30; number admitted to the Church during the past year, 10; missionary ladies connected with the school, 2; Japanese teachers, 7; grant received from the Board of Foreign Missions, yen 1200.

I would say that the outlook for our school appears encouraging. At the beginning of the last school year, April 1900, 30 pupils were enrolled; and the beginning of the present year, 45 were enrolled and the number has since increased. I personally think the prospect for girls schools is undoubtedly cheering, and the possibilities of their usefulness greater than ever before, while their need is not diminished by any other arrangements so far made for the education of Japanese girls.

I have done but little outside of school work, yet have had very intimate relations with the West Church of Osaka, and can report its membership alive and earnest. The morning Sunday-school for adults and young people carries on systematic and most enthusiastic Bible study. An afternoon Sunday-school for children is made up almost entirely of unruly street children; yet after some 10 years of such work, at last the point has been reached where from 50 to 70 such little ones crowded into a small room, can be controlled by the teachers and the lessons quietly taught. The teachers come from the Wilmina Girls School; all the Christian boarders teaching under the supervision of a lady teacher, a former graduate of the school. The women have several flourishing societies, and the men also are active in working out their own salvation and that of others.

In conclusion, I would say that I have always opportunities enough to fill the time of any three women, and there is no other woman to whom I can turn them over; for all the women stationed in Osaka are as full of work. The field is certainly white and ready for reapers but the laborers are far too few to gather in the sheaves already ripe, not to speak of the as needful labor of preparing new fields and sowing seed. Let us pray the Lord of the harvest for more laborers."

Dr. J. B. Hail:—"My work is in Wakayama Ken. In this field we have four organized churches. These churches are located at Wakayama, a city of 60,000 inhabitants; at Hikata a manufacturing town seven miles from Wakayama; at Tanabe sixty-seven miles away, an old castle town, and a county seat; and at Shingu, 150 miles down the coast also a county seat and an old castle town. In Wakayama there are four resident missionaries: one Roman Catholic, one American Episcopalian and two Cumberland Presbyterian. There are four Churches: viz. One Roman Catholic, one Greek Catholic, one Episcopal and one congregation connected with the Church of Christ in Japan. Besides the missionaries there are six paid Christian workers, four of these being Protestant. We have a workers meeting in which the Greek Church evangelist, and the Episcopal missionaries and workers and our own workers take part. This meeting is held every month and has been of great benefit to all concerned in maintaining Christian fellowship and preventing friction.

The congregation of the Church of Christ employs the Rev. Aoki for half of his time. He is employed the other half by the mission. This time he spends in visiting seven towns between Wakayama and Tanabe. These towns he visits once per month spending from one to three days in a place as the interests of the work may require. In five of these outlying towns there are Christians; in all of them inquirers.

When in the city Mr. Aoki has three Bible classes, meeting on Monday, Tuesday and Thursday evenings, besides the Sunday-school and regular preaching services on Sunday and the church prayer meeting on Friday night. Mrs. Hail and her helper have an afternoon Sunday-school at one of the preaching-places, a womans meeting on Thursday afternoon, a *Yonen Kwai* on Saturday afternoon, and a childrens meeting on Wednesday evening. Two new features of this work are (1) an all day meeting of the women once a month. The women meet at nine o'clock in the morning the second Thursday in each month. Each one brings lunch and they spend the day working, closing with a Bible lesson and prayer. The proceeds of the work go to the church. (2) The *Yonen Kwai*. The children spend an hour every week working, and the proceeds go to the Okayama Orphanage.

Outside of the regular church meetings, I am a member of two clubs. One of these is called the Wakayama English Club. It was

78

organized shortly after the coming into operation of the new treaties. The two objects of the club are the cultivation of friendly relations between Japanese and foreigners and mutual improvement. The club has a membership of about thirty and an average attendance of about ten. The meetings are opened with singing English hymns and prayer. A Bible lesson is given and then an hour of free conversation follows. The club is composed of both men and women. The second club has not yet been named. The members number only six. The object of the members of the *club* is to get English; my object is to give them religious instruction. The first hour I give to the *club*; the second hour the club gives to *me*. They use their time in getting as much English as they can; I use my hour in lecturing or free conversation or Bible reading. This is one of the most interesting meetings I have during the week. The time is Tuesday evening. On Wednesday afternoons I have a class of fifteen military officers at a town called Kada three miles from Wakayama. This is purely English. Occasionally only, the conversation in the class turns on religion. We meet in the temple; and about four o'clock we make the old temple ring with "Marching through Georgia" and "Hold the Fort." I have had several opportunities to talk in private with some of these officers. Most of them have been more or less under the tuition of missionaries before and are Christian in sentiment. On Wednesday night I lecture on Old Testament History at our preaching-place, and on Sunday night preach for the Hikate Church. House-to-house work has been kept up during the year and grows more and more interesting, especially in the homes where we have visited more than once. Our Japanese bretheren also are now taking up this work, and judging by their reports they find it very interesting. Mr. Aoki on his last ten day's trip reports fifty-six visits made; an average of more than five per day.

Representatives of the Twentieth Century Evangelistic movement visited our city and field. The church prepared the way by issuing a tract explaining briefly and simply Christianity and also notices of the meetings. The two leading daily papers and the Osaka *Asahi Shimbun* circulated these as folders in their issues. The proprietor of the *Jitsu Gyo Shimbun* placed his large hall at our service and the first meeting was held there. Meetings were also held for Christians alone, and the visiting brethren in company with our most earnest Christians visited all the members of the church and some inquirers. At the close of the public services tracts and gospels were given to any one who wished them. Those who wished to inquire further were requested to leave their names and addresses at the table where the tracts were given out. Over fifty names and addresses were given in. The pastor has had his hands full since in following up these persons. Some of our Christians who had been dead spiritually for a number of years have been attending church regularly since the visits of our brethren, and we are hoping and praying for a general revival.

Between Tanabe and Shingu are ten towns and villages visited regularly from Tanabe and seven from Shingu. These towns with only three or four exceptions have some Christian residents, and all except one have inquirers. Messrs. Ito and Maiya both report many earnest inquirers. The Airin church has held its own. They have no

79

pastor or evangelist living with them; but the members have all been faithful. There are now some very earnest inquirers among the young men. This church also has had a visit from the men sent out by the Evangelical Alliance Committee, and also from Mr. Hoshino who was sent by the Synod. The meeting was held in the largest theatre in the town. The house was full, the preaching evangelical, and the attention earnest. The visible result has been larger audiences and more serious attention at the regular church services, and the little band of Christians greatly cheered."

MISS ELLA GARDNER:—"My special work has been a weekly lesson with the Christian women; a class in the Sunday-school of 16 girls: two weekly classes for children in different parts of the town. The latter classes have added numbers to the Sunday-school, and have been the means of preparing the way to teaching the women of the neighborhood, a number of whom have stayed for a lesson, after the childrens meeting was over. Three women have become interested enough to attend the womans Bible class.

Mr. Worley has the superintendence of the Sunday-school for a year, and we have quite an up-to-date school. In the past year it has more than doubled its membership. We have made several trips into the country, for the purpose of strengthening the faith of isolated Christians, and helping those who are studying the Bible. Wherever we have gone, the people are anxious to hear the gospel. Our Christians are planning to rebuild their church."

MR. WORLEY:—"My work last fall in Tsu consisted of a class in Sunday-school, and teaching some English at home. After coming to Shingu, I began to make some evangelistic trips with Mr. Mameya. We made several trips to Kinomoto, and I went once as far as Ise, stopping at Owashi, Nagashima and Toba. For several months we had regular weekly meetings in Kumanoji, as well as in the western part of Shingu. At Kinomoto and Owashi, there are several men who are studying the Bible, and show a true desire of becoming Christians. From the first of the year I have been leading the Sunday-school of the Shingu church. Mrs. Worley had two childrens meetings during the week for four or five months, and still continues the one in Kumanoji. There was an average attendance of one hundred children. She also has had a class of boys in the church school, since the first of the year."

MRS. DRENNAN:—"The past year in my work has so much in common with the work and report made every year, that it is difficult to know what to write and what to omit. Among the important meetings of the year, I would mention our annual womans meeting in April last, which really deserves the enomium usually given to such meetings. viz. the best one we have held. There was a good attendance, marked by its spirituality, which grew more manifest as the meeting advanced in the discussion of the subject Following Jesus. The different topics in the following partial program were discussed with deep interest and feeling. Following Christ.—What is it to follow Christ? How can we follow Him? When must we follow Christ?

80

Where must we follow Him? In what must we follow Him? The privilege of following Christ. The cost of following Him. The reward of following Him. Papers were read on each topic, after which talks and prayers followed promptly. Discussing such a subject as these with Bible reading, prayers, and spiritual songs, could scarcely fail to produce good in the hearts of those who heard. "God was with us" was the general expression of all. I think I have seen the fruit of it manifest in the deepened spiritual life of the women of our church. And I hope I did not fail to receive a portion of the blessing so richly enjoyed by others. One hour was given to the children, one hour to the old ladies, and one to the temperance and social purity question.

Soon after the meeting we were called upon to mourn the death of our dearly beloved brother, Yonemori; one of the most consecrated, earnest workers I have ever known. He will doubtless be remembered, as the first convert of the Ueno work, who after years of consecrated Christian living was set apart by prayer to lay-evangelistic work; ever afterwards doing faithfully that work, until called in triumph to lay down his armor. But his works do follow.

The next event out of the ordinary was the marriage of one of our Bible women to the present pastor of the Yokkaichi church. Our prayers go with her that she may be as useful in her new relation of life as she was in the past.

Our Sabbath-school work is in good condition. A regular attendance, during the past year, of from forty to fifty children. Also a Bible class of from twenty to twenty-five grown persons. Preaching and prayer meeting services are well attended. There have been eighteen adults and nine children baptized. This gives us 70 adult members and 19 children.

From our Treasurer's report, I find, by regular monthly contributions, they meet all running expenses of the church, repairs on house, fence, presbyterial and synodical dues, contributions to the Home Mission Board and pay five yen per month on their pastor's salary; besides having purchased an organ. Yet we have no wealthy ones among us, and the majority of our members are women.

Our Bible school has been at work as usual. Girls and Bible women, supported the past year by individuals and societies in America, have enabled me to keep the girls in school; besides keeping up needed repairs, furniture and books for our school, Sunday-school papers, etc. Two societies in America supply Bibles for our meetings, and the expenses of one of our preaching places. One of our Bible women is at work in Ueno, one is assisting in teaching in the school, another doing Bible work here. Our Bible class for men is kept up as usual every Sabbath afternoon. Two of those received into the church this month are from this class, four from the old ladies class. Meetings for young women and for old women are kept up regularly as before, and with deepening interest. I think all of our meetings are growing more spiritual. There is a readiness to hear the gospel more than we have ever known in this province.

In the early part of the year, I was in bed with a severe case of grippe. Before recovering entirely, a cold caused a relapse, from which I was slow to recover. However through April I was at my work, and able to arrange for and conduct our annual womens meeting.

I was compelled however, to leave off work when the heat of June came on. Mr. Worley kindly took my class of young men, teaching them until the close of the month. I took my summer vacation principally in bed; but with the fall, again took up my regular work, this time greatly assisted by Mr. Preston, who while resting here through the perilous times in China, busied himself with what his hand could find to do, a great blessing indeed to me and to our work. It gave me rest and time for other extra work, in preparing our Sunday-school pupils for their usual Christmas exercises.

In looking back over the work of the year, I am filled with gratitude. All along the line of our work I can see some progress. It seems as if the Lord had laid his hand upon me, and shut me out from care and work, thus telling me to see the work is not brought forward by earthly power, by human skill or zeal, be it ever so earnest, but by his Spirit. I was made to see and feel that the work is his. He will provide."

MISS LEAVITT:—"In reporting for Tanabe for the past year, I have little that is new to tell. The methods used are the same. The conditions are not greatly changed from those given a year ago. The most hopeful indication is the increased number of inquirers. There are now eight persons who say that they wish to be come Christians, and several others, who with them are studying the Bible in a class held for them, besides attending the general meetings. Some of these persons were first interested by the visit from the Okayama Orphanage band, and Mr. Ishii, stereopticon lectures. One woman said she really thought till then that Christianity was an evil teaching. During the last year, ten members were added to the church, of whom four were baptized on profession of faith; one young man and three women. Two of the latter were wives of Christian men.

Two women, members of the Episcopal Church, who had been working cordially with us for a long while, separated themselves from all of our meetings after the arrival of an evangelist of their own denomination.

The weekly meeting for women has been changed a little. At one meeting in the month, helpful subjects of general interest are discussed. They have had talks given by various persons, on religion, education, hygiene, cooking, care of children. These meetings have an attendance of from thirty to fifty. The Bible lessons given the other three weeks, have about half that number. The womans class in Sunday-school has usually 1500 20 present, about double the number of men. At the night service, the house is full on the women's side, while there is spare room across the aisle. The childrens Sunday-school had 97 enrolled, with an average attendance of 55. We have secured a good teacher for the intermediate grade, one whose pupils are able to tell what they are taught. The work has been as helpful to the teacher as she has been to the class. A knitting class has been held once a week. A small fee is charged, and a short Bible lesson given at the end of the work hour. The average attendance has been about forty-five; mostly girls from 10 years old upward.

I have done no evangelistic work outside of Tanabe, except that incidental to a trip with Miss Gardner to Shingu, and on other trips on the boat to and from Osaka. A little child was left in my care last spring under circumstances which made it almost impossible to refuse the charge. I have tried to make use of this opportunity to teach by example something of right training for children, because it seems sadly lacking, and little understood by the Japanese. With this in view, I felt justified in giving some little time to the child, which might have otherwise been spent in outside work.

Attending the Tokyo Conference, and building, have hindered my work somewhat but will prove a help in the long run. So much can hardly be said of a month of poor health, which upset some plans for work. Considering the faithfulness of the pastor, the good fellowship of all the church members, the full meetings and large numbers of outsiders, who are now more or less interested, I have never had a more hopeful outlook to report for Tanabe."

III.

APPENDIX

I.

CONSTITUTION

OF THE

PROPOSED STANDING COMMITTEE OF CO-OPERATING CHRISTIAN MISSIONS IN JAPAN.

ARTICLE 1. NAME.

This Committee shall be called The Standing Committee of Co-operating Christian Missions in Japan.

ARTICLE 2. FUNCTIONS.

1. This Committee shall serve as a general medium of reference, communication and effort for the co-operating missions in matters of common interest and in co-operative enterprises. On application of interested parties, and in cases of urgent importance on its own initiative, the Committee may give counsel:

    a With regard to the distribution of forces for evangelistic, educational and eleemosynary work, especially where enlargement is contemplated;

    b With regard to plans for union or co-operation on the part of two or more missions for any or all of the above forms of missionary work;

    c And in general with a view to the prevention of misunderstandings and the promotion of harmony of spirit and uniformity of method among the co-operating missions.

84

2. The work of this Committee may include :

   a The formation of plans calculated to stimulate the production and circulation of Christian literature ;

   b The arranging for special evangelistic campaigns, for the services of visitors from abroad as preachers or lecturers, and for other forms of co-operative evangelistic effort;

   c In securing joint action to meet emergencies affecting the common interests of the co-operating missions.

   d In serving as a means of communication between the co-operating missions the Committee shall be authorized to publish at least once a year a record of social and religions conditions and progress.

Article 3. Composition.

1. This Committee shall be composed of representatives of as many of the evangelical Christian missions in Japan as may choose to co-operate with it on the following basis, to wit :

   a Each mission having fifteen (15) members, inclusive of the wives of missionaries, shall be entitled to one representative with full powers, such representative to be called a full member ;

   b Each mission having forty-five (45) members shall be entitled to two representatives with full powers ;

   c Each mission · having seventy-five (75) members, or more, shall be entitled to three representatives with full powers ;

   d Any mission having a membership of not less than five (5) shall be entitled to representation by one corresponding member, who shall possess all the rights of full members, except that of voting.

2. Two or more missions without regard to their size may at discretion combine to form a group. In such cases each group shall, so far as the purposes of this Committee are concerned, be counted as a mission, and shall be entitled to representation accordingly.

3. The full members and the corresponding members shall be the media of communication between the Committee and the missions, or groups of missions, which they respectively represent.

4. The members of this Committee shall be chosen by the missions, or groups of missions, which they respectively represent, or shall be appointed by the proper authorities in their respective missions or groups, to serve for such terms as said missions or groups may individually determine.

Article 4. Withdrawal.

A mission may at any time withdraw from co-operation with the Committee by notifying the Secretary in writing of its decision to do so.

Article 5. Officers.

The officers of this Committee shall be a Chairman, a Vice-chairman, a Secretary and a Treasurer, who shall hold office for one year, or until their successors are elected. They shall be chosen by ballot.

ARTICLE 6. MEETINGS.

1. Regular meetings of the Committee shall be held annually at such times and places as the Committee shall determine. Special meetings may be held at any time at the call of the Chairman, or, if he be unable to act, the Vice-chairman, in case five or more full members representing at least three missions, or groups of missions, shall so desire.

2. A quorum for the transaction of business shall include representatives from at least two-thirds, of the co-operating missions, or groups of missions, having full members.

ARTICLE 7. EXPENSES.

1. The ordinary expenses of this Committee, including the cost of attendance of full members on its meetings, shall, up to the sum of *yen* 500 per annum, be met by the several missions represented by full members in proportion to such representation.

2. Extraordinary expenses shall be incurred only as special provision may be made by the missions or otherwise for meeting them.

ARTICLE 8. AMENDMENTS.

Amendments to this constitution may be proposed at any time either by the Committee or by any one of the co-operating missions, and said amendments shall take effect when the missions represented by not less than three-fourths of the full members for the Committee shall have given notice to the Secretary of their consent.

ARTICLE 9. ORGANIZATION.

1. This constitution shall go into effect when such a number of the missions as include in their membership (the wives of missionaries included not less than two-thirds of the Protestant missionaries in Japan shall have signified their acceptance of the same in writing to the Secretary of the so called Promoting Committee.

2. When the conditions of the foregoing section are fulfilled, the Chairman of the Promoting Committee shall issue a call for the first meeting of The Standing Committee of Co-operating Missions in Japan, not less than two months in advance of the date fixed for the meeting.

3. It shall be the duty of the Chairman of the Promoting Committee, or, if he be unable to act, the Secretary, to attend the first meeting mentioned in the foregoing section, and to preside until a permanent organization is effected.

II

Regulations for the Admission of Students to the Government High Schools*

The new regulations regarding the admission of students to the Government High Schools (Koto Gakko), as published in the *Official Gazette* of May 7-9, are as follows:—

1. Those who are still students in a Chu Gakko, or a school recognized by the Department of Education as of a grade equal to or above that of a Chu Gakko established by the Government (or by a *Fu* or *Ken*, in accordance with Regulation No. 34, Art. 2, Section 3, in the thirty-second year of Meiji), may not apply for admission. This however does not apply to post graduate students.

2. Those who apply for the preliminary examination shall send in a written application by the thirty-first of this month (May). Those who are not required to pass the preliminary examination shall send their application to the Koto Gakko which they desire to enter before the fifth of June. The application shall state which Department the student desires to enter and give his history as a student. It shall also be accompanied with his photograph; and, in the case of a graduate of a Chu Gakko or a school recognized by the Department of Education as of a grade equal to or above that of a Chu Gakko (as described above), with a certificate from the Principal of such school.

The form of application is as follows:—

To the President of ——— Koto Gakko:

I desire to enter the Preparatory Department of your school; and beg leave herewith to state which Department I wish to enter, and to forward my history, photograph, a certificate from the ——— School (This is confined to those who are graduates of a Chu Gakko, or a school recognized by the Department of Education as of a grade equal to or above that of a Chu Gakko, as described above), and also the fee for the competitive entrance examination.

3. Place of examination.

The application for the entrance examination may be sent to any Koto Gakko; but it shall state which particular school the applicant desires to enter. He need not however go to that school in order to be examined.

---

* Translation of *Japan Mail.*

4. Kinds of examination.

Preliminary examination. This examination is required of those applicants who are not graduates of a Chu Gakko or a school recognized by the Department of Education as of a grade equal to or above that of a Chu Gakko (as described above).

Competitive examination. This examination shall be required when the number of applicants who are graduates of the Chu Gakko or of schools recognized by the Department of Education as of a grade equal to or above that of a Chu Gakko (as described above), and who have passed the preliminiary examination, exceeds the number determined upon for entrance to the several Koto Gakko.

5. Subjects for examination and extent required.

The preliminary examination shall include all the subjects prescribed for the Chu Gakko. The other examination shall include Japanese and Chinese, a foreign language, history, mathematics, physics and chemistry; and in all these to the extent required in the Chu Gakko, as laid down by the Department of Education in Regulations Nos. 14 and 7 and issued respectively in the nineteenth and the twenty-seventh year of Meiji. The foreign language for all the Koto Gakko shall be English. In the case of those, however, who wish to enter the French Law or Literature Department in the Tokyo Koto Gakko, it may be French; and in the case of those who wish to enter the German Law or Literature Department, or the Department of Medicine, it may be German.

6. Examination fees.

The examination fee shall be sent in with the application. Those however who apply for the preliminary examination need not pay the fee for the competitive examination until after passing the preliminary examination. The fees are as follows:—For the preliminary examination, yen 5; for the competitive examination yen 3, for the Tokyo Koto Gakko; and yen 2 for the other Koto Gakko.

7. Time of the examinations.

The preliminary examination will be held from June third; the competitive examination from July third.

Other particulars may be obtained by writing to a Koto Gakko prior to the day for examination.

The numbers of students that will be admitted this year to the entering classes of the several Koto Gakko, according to Departments, are as follows:—Tokyo, a. 160, b. 105, c. 70; Sendai, a. 80, b. 61, c. 35; Kyoto, a. 70, b. 70, c. 85; Kanazawa, a. 85. b. 85, c. 35; Kumamoto, a. 110, b. 70, c. 35; Okayama, a. 70, b. 70, c. 35; Yamaguchi, a. 75, b. 70, c. 35.

IV.

ROLL OF THE COUNCIL.

EAST JAPAN MISSION OF THE PRESBYTERIAN
CHURCH IN THE U.S.A. (NORTHERN).

Ballagh, Mr. J.C.,* 1875† . . . . . . Tokyo.
Ballagh, Mrs. J.C.. 1884 . . . (in U.S.) ,,
Haworth, Rev. B.C., 1887 . . . (,, ,,) ,,
Haworth, Mrs. B.C. . . . . . (,, ,,) ,,
Imbrie, Rev. William, D.D , 1875 . . . ,,
Imbrie, Mrs. William . . . . ,,
Landis, Rev. H.M.,* 1888 . . . . . ,,
Landis, Mrs. H.M.* . . . . ,,
MacNair, Rev. T.M.,* 1883 . . . . ,,
MacNair, Mrs. T.M.,* 1880. . . . . ,,
Pierson, Rev. G.P., 1888 . . . . . . Asahigawa.
Pierson, Mrs. G.P., 1891. . . . . . ,,
Thompson, Rev. David, D.D., 1863 . . . Tokyo.
Thompson, Mrs. David, 1873 . . . . . ,,

Ballagh, Miss A.P., 1884. . . . (in U.S.) Tokyo.
Case, Miss E.W.,* 1887 . . . . Yokohama.
Gardner, Miss Sarah, 1889 . . . . . Tokyo.
McCauley, Mrs. J.K.,* 1880 . . . . . ,,

* Present at the meeting of the Council in Karuizawa, August 1901.
† Year of arrival in Japan.

Milliken, Miss Elizabeth P., 1884 . . . Tokyo.
Rose, Miss C.H., 1886 . . . .(in U.S.) Otaru.
Smith, Miss S.C., 1880 . . . . Sapporo.
Wells, Miss Lilian, 1900. . . . . . . ,,
West, Miss A.B., 1883 . . . .(in U.S.) Tokyo.
Wyckoff, Miss Helena 1901. . . . . . ,,
Youngman, Miss K.M., 1873 . . . . . ,,

WEST JAPAN MISSION OF THE PRESBYTERIAN
CHURCH IN THE U.S.A. (NORTHERN).

Alexander, Rev. T.T., D.D.,* 1877 . . . Kyoto.
Alexander, Mrs. T.T. . . . .(in U.S.) ,,
Ayres, Rev. J.B.,* 1888 . . . . Yamaguchi.
Ayres, Mrs. J.B.,*. . . . . . . ,,
Brokaw, Rev. H.,* 1896 . . . . . Hiroshima.
Brokaw, Mrs. H.* . . . . . ,,
Bryan, Rev. A.V., 1882. . . . Matsuyama.
Bryan, Mrs. A.V., 1887. . . . ,,
Curtis, Rev, F.S., 1887 . . . . Yamaguchi.
Curtis, Mrs. F.S. . . . . . . ,,
Doughty, Rev. J.W., 1890 . . . Hiroshima.
Doughty, Mrs. J.W. . . . . . ,,
Dunlop, Rev. J.G. 1890 . . . . Kanazawa.
Dunlop, Mrs. J.G., 1894 . . ,,
Fulton, Rev. G.W. . . . . ,,
Fulton, Mrs. G.W. . . . . . ,,
Jones, Rev. W.Y.,* 1895 . . Fukui.
Jones, Mrs. W.Y.,* 1884 . . ,,
Winn, Rev. T.C.,* 1878 . . Osaka.
Winn, Mrs. T.C.* . . . . ,,

Bigelow, Miss G.S.,* 1886 . . Yamaguchi.
Garvin, Miss A.E.,* 1882 . . . Osaka.
Glenn, Miss Grace Curtis 1898 . . . Kanazawa.
Haworth, Miss Alice, 1888 . . . . . . Kyoto.
Kelly, Miss M.E., 1893 . . .(in U.S.) ,,
Luther, Miss Ida R., 1898 . . . Kanazawa.
Mayo, Miss Lucy E., 1901 . . . ,,

90

Nivling, Miss Marion, 1899 . . . . Hiroshima.
Palmer, Miss M.M., 1892 . . . . . Yamaguchi.
Porter, Miss F.E., 1882 . . . . in U.S.) Kanazawa.
Settlemeyer, Miss E., 1893 . . . (,, ,,) Kyoto.
Shaw, Miss Kate, 1889 . . . . Kanazawa.
Ward, Miss Isabel Mae, 1901 . . . . . Osaka.

NORTH JAPAN MISSION OF THE REFORMED
(DUTCH) CHURCH IN AMERICA.

Ballagh, Rev. J.H.,* 1861 . . . . Yokohama.
Ballagh, Mrs. J.H. . . . . ,,
Booth, Rev. Eugene S.,* 1879 . . . . ,,
Booth, Mrs. Eugene S.* . . . . ,,
Harris, Rev. Howard, 1883 . . (in U.S.) Aomori.
Harris, Mrs. Howard . . . . (,, ,,) ,,
Miller, Rev. E. Rothesay,* 1872 . . . . Morioka.
Miller, Mrs. E. Rothesay,* 1870 . . . . ,,
Scudder, Rev. Frank S.,* 1897 . . . . Nagano.
Scudder, Mrs. Frank S.* . . . . . . ,,
Wyckoff, M.N., D.Sc.,* 1881 . . . . . Tokyo.
Wyckoff, Mrs. M.N.* . . . . ,,

Deyo, Miss Mary, 1888 . . . . (in U.S.) Ueda.
Moulton, Miss Julia, 1891 . . . . . Yokohama.
Schenck, Mrs. J.W., 1897 . . . (in U.S.) Nagano.
Thompson, Miss Anne De F., 1887 . . . Yokohama.
Winn, Miss L., 1881 . . . . Aomori.
Wyckoff, Miss Harriet J.,* 1898 . . . . ,,

SOUTH JAPAN MISSION OF THE REFORMED
(DUTCH) CHURCH IN AMERICA.

Myers, Rev. C.M., 1899 . . . . . . Nagasaki.
Oltmans, Rev. Albert,* 1886 . . . . . Saga.
Oltmans, Mrs. Albert . . . . . . ,,
Peeke, Rev. H.V.S., 1893 . . . . Kagoshima.
Peeke, Mrs. H.V.S. . . . . ,,
Pieters, Rev. Albertus, 1891 . . . . ,,

91

Pieters, Mrs. Albertus . . . . Kagoshima.
Stout, Rev. Henry, D.D., 1869 . Nagasaki.
Stout, Mrs. Henry . . . . . „

Couch, Miss Sara M., 1892 . . (in U.S.) Nagasaki.
Lansing, Miss Harriet M., 1893 . . . . Kagoshima.
Stout, Miss A.B., 1898 . . . . Nagasaki.

MISSION OF THE PRESBYTERIAN CHURCH IN THE U.S. (SOUTHERN).

Buchanan, Rev. W.C., 1891 . . . . . Takamatsu.
Buchanan, Mrs. W.C. . . . . „
Buchanan, Rev. Walter McS.,* 1895 . . „
Buchanan, Mrs. Walter McS.,* 1887 . . „
Cumming, Rev. C.K., 1889 . . . . . Nagoya.
Cumming, Mrs. C.K., 1892 . . . . . „
Fulton, Rev. S.P., 1888 . . . . . . Tokyo.
Fulton, Mrs. S.P. . . . . „
Hope, Rev. S.R., 1892 . . . . . .
Hope, Mrs. S.R. . . . .
McAlpine, Rev. R.E., 1885 . . . . . Nagoya.
McAlpine, Mrs. R.E. . . . . „
McIlvaine, Bev. W.B.,* 1889 . . . . Kochi.
McIlvaine, Mrs. W.B. . . . . . „
Moore, Rev. J.B., 1890 . . . . . . Susaki.
Moore, Mrs. J.B., 1893 . . . . . . „
Myers, Rev. H.W.,* 1897 . . . . . . Tokushima.
Myers, Mrs. H.W.* . . . . „
Price, Rev. H.B.* 1887 . . . . . . Kobe.
Price, Mrs. H.B., 1890 . . . . . . „

Dowd, Miss Annie,* 1887 . . . . . . Kobe.
Evans, Miss Sala, 1893 . . . (in U.S.) Kochi.
Houston, Miss Ella,* 1891 . . . . . Nagoya.
Moore, Miss Elizabeth, 1894 . . (in U.S.) „
Patton, Miss A.V.* . . . . Tokushima.
Patton, Miss Florence,* 1895 . . . . „

92

Sterling, Miss Charlotte E., 1887 (in U.S.) . Kochi.
Wimbish, Miss Elizabeth, 1887 . . . . . Nagoya.

MISSION OF THE REFORMED (GERMAN) CHURCH IN THE U.S.

Faust, Rev. A.K.,* 1900 . . . . . . Sendai.
Gerhard, Mr. Paul L., 1897 . . (in U.S.) „
Lampe, Rev. W.E.,* 1900 . . . . . . „
Lampe, Mrs. W.E.* . . . . „
Miller, Rev. H.K., 1892 . . . . . . Yamagata.
Miller, Mrs. H.K. . . . . „
Moore, Rev. J.P., D.D., 1883 . (in U.S.) Tokyo.
Moore, Mrs. J.P. . . . . . . („ „) „
Noss, Rev. C., 1895 . . . . Sendai.
Noss, Mrs. C. . . . . „
Schneder, Rev. D.B., D.D., 1887 . . . „
Schneder, Mrs. D.B. . . . . „
Snyder, Rev. S.S.* 1894 . . . . . . „
Snyder, Mrs. S.S.* . . . . „

Pifer, Miss Catharine . . . . Sendai.
Powell, Miss Lucy M., 1900 . . . . . „
Weidner, Miss Sadie Lea,* 1900 . . . . „
Zurfluh, Miss Lena, 1894 . . . (in U.S.) „

MISSION OF THE CUMBERLAND PRESBYTERIAN CHURCH.

Hail, Rev. A.D., D.D., 1878 . . . , . Osaka.
Hail, Mrs. A.D. . . . . „
Hail, Rev. J.B., D.D.,* 1877 . . . . . Wakayama.
Hail, Mrs. J.B. . . . . „
Hail, Rev. J.E.,* 1900 . . . . Osaka.
Hudson, Rev. G.G., 1886 . . . (in U.S.) „
Hudson, Mrs. G.G. . . . . . („ „) „
Van Horne, Rev. G.W.,* 1888 . . . . „
Van Horne, Mrs. G.W.* . . . . . . „
Worley, Rev. J.C., 1899 . . . . . . Tsu.
Worley, Mrs. J.C. . . . . „

Alexander, Miss S., 1894 . . . . Osaka (?)
Drennan, Mrs. A.M., 1883 . . . . . . Tsu.
Gardner, Miss Ella,* 1893 . . . . Tanabe.
Leavitt, Miss Julia, 1881 . . . (in U.S.) ,,
Lyons, Mrs. N.A., 1894 . . . (,, ,,) Osaka.
Morgan, Miss Agnes E.,* 1889 . . . . ,,
Ransom, Miss 1901 . . . . ,,

WOMANS UNION MISSIONARY SOCIETY.

Berninger, Miss Martha, 1900. . . . . Yokohama.
Crosby, Miss Julia N., 1871 . . . . . ,,
Hand, Miss Julia E., 1900 . . . . . . ,,
Pratt, Miss S.A., 1893 . . . . .(in U.S.) ,,
Strain, Miss Helen Knox 1900 . . . . ,,